COPPER

COPPER

Rebecca Lisle

G. P. Putnam's Sons ❧ New York

For Rina Vergano

Library of Congress Cataloging-in-Publication Data
Lisle, Rebecca.   Copper / Rebecca Lisle.—1st American ed.   p.   cm.   Summary: Pursued
by enemies of the family she never knew she had, ten-year-old Copper Beech flees
to Spindle House, her paternal home, and decides to uncover the truth about a feud
between the Stone and Wood clans that sent her into exile six years earlier. [1. Vendetta—
Fiction. 2. Family—Fiction. 3. Magic—Fiction. 4. Toys—Fiction. 5. Adventure and
adventurers—Fiction.] I. Title.   PZ7.L6913Co 2004   [Fic]—dc21   2003005973
ISBN 0-399-24211-2
10 9 8 7 6 5 4 3 2 1
First Impression

Contents

Part One: The Ordinary Place

1. Leaving   2
2. How Copper Left   5
3. Copper's Birthday   11
4. The Journey   18

Part Two: The Marble Mountains

5. Spindle House   26
6. The First Day   29
7. Robin and Oriole   34
8. The Rockers   39
9. Wood and Stone   45
10. Uncle Greenwood   50
11. More Clues   58
12. Sledding   65
13. Looking for the Room at the Top of the House   73
14. Copper Investigates the Dumbwaiter   79
15. Copper Runs Away   81

PART THREE: INSIDE THE ROCK

16. Granite   90
17. Granite's Secret   101
18. Amber   107
19. Across the Lake   117
20. Home Again   126
21. An Extraordinary Block of Ice   135
22. Copper Has to Go Back to the Rock   140
23. Locked in the Rock   147
24. The Mystery of the Green Vapor   155
25. The Truth About Great-Grandfather Ash   160
26. Brother and Sister   165
27. Copper Knows What She Wants to Knit
      for the First Time   175

PART ONE

THE ORDINARY PLACE

1. LEAVING

"PHEW! MADE IT." Copper collapsed into her train seat. The train was due to leave in three minutes. "Made it, made it," she repeated breathlessly. "Now please, train, go!"

The train carriage alongside hers shifted slowly past, and for a second Copper's heart raced expectantly, thinking *she* was moving, but then the platform across the rails came into view and she realized what had happened.

Hurry, hurry, she urged. We must go. We must get away.

She stared nervously through the train window at the gray mass of people and suddenly she saw them: even though she'd never seen them before, even though she didn't know what they looked like, she knew it was *them*.

She squashed back in her seat and slithered down out of sight, peeping at the men from below the safety of the window ledge.

They looked foreign; out of context in the busy station. They were bundled in heavy coats and scarves and big boots.

Their hair was long and tangled. Their skin was gray, as if they'd been living under a stone with the worms.

Up and down they paced, like lions stalking prey, and there was an intensity in their wild stares that sent a shiver up Copper's back.

Don't let them see me, don't let them, please.

The massive digital clock above the platform showed there were now only thirty-three seconds to go. They couldn't reach her now, could they? She peeped round the edge of the window.

They were staring intently at the other travelers, scrutinizing them, then turning away in disgust. Copper thought she could hear them shouting, "That's not her! That's not her!" their angry voices rising above the roar of the station.

Suddenly the shorter man lunged at a small girl with red hair. He dragged her close, thrusting his face into hers. The girl screamed; her parents grabbed her, and at the same moment, a whistle blew shrilly and the two men turned and ran, just as Copper's train eased slowly out of the station with a long metallic squeal.

Copper breathed again. "Safe," she whispered, sitting up again and relaxing her tensed arms and legs.

"Oi, that's my nose!" said a small voice from underneath her.

"Oh, Ralick, sorry," Copper whispered. She looked round anxiously, but no one was watching her, so she pulled Ralick out and sat him on the arm of the seat. She had to be careful no one saw her talking to a toy: they'd think she was mad. "How did you get under me like that?"

"How did you get on top of me like that, you mean."

Copper hushed him gently. "Shh, shh, someone will hear you. I saw them! They were there, Ralick: the men Aunt Ruby told me about. They followed us."

"Dang! I wish I'd seen them. Wish I'd got my hands on those scoundrels. I may be a stuffed toy, but I'm full of fight," said Ralick proudly. "What about you? Are you all right? You look all wobbly."

"I feel a bit wobbly," Copper admitted. "Frayed at the edges. I'm sort of excited and sad and scared all in one go. I'll try knitting; it usually helps." She pulled the ball of blue wool out of her pocket and cast on some stitches. "How will Aunt Ruby be managing without us?"

"Very well, I expect, since she was the one who sent us away," said Ralick.

"She didn't want to," said Copper.

She began knitting. Automatically the wool slipped round: pearl one, knit one, pearl one, knit one, and as the rhythm of the train and the rhythm of her knitting flowed together, her thoughts drifted back to the peculiar events that had brought her to that train on that evening, running from everything she'd ever known.

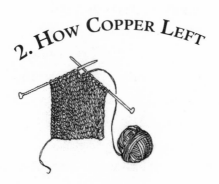

2. How Copper Left

"I'd like to have a wolf," said Copper.

She was curled up on the old sofa by the fire in her aunt's studio with a book on her lap, watching Aunt Ruby work on a sculpture. "It says in this book that wolves are one of the most faithful animals in the world."

"Wolves?" Aunt Ruby's chisel clattered to the floor. "Goodness, Copper, what are you talking about *wolves* for?" Aunt Ruby noisily blew some fine dust from the curves of her sculpture. "A wolf? You want a wolf?"

"Yes. It says they're very loyal creatures." She put her book down. "Loyal forever . . . I'd like a wolf."

"Ridiculous, my lamb," said Aunt Ruby, "although I did have a dragon once and she was loyal. . . . You know how ducks get fixated on things? The first object they see when they hatch—that's mum, whether it's a bucket or a duck or a piece of paper. Dragons do that too and luckily mine saw me. Dragons are intelligent too."

"Aunt Ruby! What a lie. You *couldn't* have had a dragon."

"I did. Just a teeny silvery green one called Glinty, though of course she would have grown big by now. Dragons are more faithful than wolves and she was wonderful at keeping me snug at night, puffing warm breath over me."

"What happened to her?"

"It was awful . . . ," said Aunt Ruby, staring into the fire. "I've tried not to think about her all these years. . . . I had a terrible fight with my brother—we argued all the time—and he dropped her down some dried-up old well."

"That's so cruel!"

"And poor Glinty, she was too young to fly, her wings weren't fully developed. I suppose she died, but I could never find out. I didn't even know where the well was, though I looked and looked. . . . I never forgave my brother for that."

"I bet you didn't . . . but is it really true? Is it all true?"

But her aunt was finished with that topic. "Now, now," she said, tucking the chisel into a pocket on her apron. "That's enough of that." She stood back to admire her work. "What do you think of this sculpture?"

Copper knew her aunt was not going to talk about dragons again. Aunt Ruby often hinted of a place where dragons and wolves lived, where things were strangely, magically different, but her stories ended suddenly, leaving Copper desperate to know more.

Reluctantly Copper turned her attention to the beautiful stone carving of a lion's head that her aunt was working on.

"It's brilliant. He looks really noble and kind. I'd like to have a lion too."

"Hmm, that would be fun." Aunt Ruby fingered the large orange beads round her neck thoughtfully.

Copper watched the firelight shining on her aunt, glimmering on her black hair and the sequins and beads on her emerald skirt.

Copper loved her aunt, adored her, even though Aunt Ruby was odd, odder than any other aunt that Copper had ever met, anyway. Which other aunt had wild, jet black hair knotted with scarves into a magnificent pile on her head? Who else wore large beads made from strange, exotic stones and shining minerals never seen anywhere else?

And Aunt Ruby was a sculptor. Copper didn't know any other aunts who were sculptors or who had, like Aunt Ruby, a special apron with thirty-nine pockets, one for each of her sharp carving tools. She was certainly the only aunt who had ever carved the stone gateposts of an ordinary little house into eagles and the lintel above the door into a dragon.

"We are a bit different from other people," she admitted to Copper, "but we must be glad of that, not ashamed. You see, we don't come from here. We've got rock and wood and the ice from the mountains coursing through our veins. We are earth people. We can make things; we've got the knowledge. You'll understand when you're older."

"Older? I'm nearly ten now," said Copper, "and I don't have any knowledge of anything. I can't use a chisel or a hammer without bashing my fingers and anyway, I don't think I want to be different. Do I want rocks and twigs in me? Earthy people sound dull and muddy."

"They're wonderful," said Aunt Ruby dreamily.

But Copper wasn't so sure. She was thinking about school. What fun was there in being different if it meant the other children ignored you or laughed at you and no one was your friend?

"You can't change what you are," said Aunt Ruby. "You're better than anyone at knitting, and I bet if that useless school of yours taught you sensible things like woodwork, you'd be top of the class at that!"

Copper made a face. She didn't think so.

Aunt Ruby was right about them being different, though. Aunt Ruby had purple eyes like amethysts, wild black hair and skin as white as paper.

And Copper with her long red hair and creamy skin, she was different too.

Plus, Copper knitted.

Instead of a small bag to carry her books and keys in, Copper carried a long knitting-needle bag. Instead of pens and pencils jutting out of her blazer pocket, she had crochet hooks. She had every type of knitting needle—wooden, metal and colored plastic—and every size. She had all types of wool too, thick and lumpy and thin and hairy. Copper knitted all the time, but she never finished anything. She *couldn't* finish anything. Her sweaters had one sleeve, her doilies never grew beyond the size of a coin, her socks got as far as the turn in the heel and then she abandoned them.

"I'm like this old three-fingered glove here. Incomplete,"

she explained to Ralick. "I'm half finished and all filled up with funny feelings."

"We all are," said Ralick. "Plus, I've got woolly fillings filling me too."

"I know everyone has feelings," said Copper, "but not like mine. I used to think it was normal to feel undone like this, as if someone started me but never finished me, but no one else feels like this, I've asked them. I'm like a half-drawn picture."

"Like a teapot without a spout?" put in Ralick.

"Exactly."

"Like a chocolate éclair without any chocolate?"

"Yes . . . Ralick, you're teasing me! But honestly, I just don't feel right. . . . And everyone else at school has at least one mother and father if not several, and dozens of half- or step-sisters or brothers and I've only got Aunt Ruby . . . and you. And actually, you're a whole family rolled into one."

Ralick growled gently to show he was pleased.

"There's nobody quite like you, Ralick."

Ralick agreed. He had brown fur rubbed bare in places and he had stiff, sticking-out legs. His nose was pointed and so were his ears, and he might have been a dog or a bear or a tiger with no stripes—it was hard to say what sort of animal he was. He had round black eyes, set rather close together, which looked glassy to ordinary people, but to Copper were full of life.

Having Ralick was another way in which Copper felt

special: no one else had a talking cuddly toy, unless, perhaps, they didn't own up to it.

There was the mystery of her birthdays too.

Each year, somebody sent her a tiny gold charm that was so beautifully made, so intricate and delicate, that when Copper was very young, she'd imagined they were made by fairies. For years Copper thought that all little girls got a gold charm for their birthday and was surprised to find they didn't. Then as she got older, Copper was sure that the charms were sent to her by her mother. A mother who loved her and knew where she was but was kept apart from her by some cruel twist of fate.

Copper felt sure Aunt Ruby knew something about them, but Aunt Ruby fended off any questions with a smile and a firm shake of her head.

Whenever Copper felt particularly incomplete (she called it her unraveled feeling), she would knit and knit and knit until she'd knitted herself back together again.

Copper and Ralick and Aunt Ruby were happy together until Copper's tenth birthday, which is really when everything changed.

3. COPPER'S BIRTHDAY

ON THE MORNING of Copper's tenth birthday, Aunt Ruby rushed into Copper's bedroom.

"Darling, are you all right?"

Copper struggled to sit up, blinking and shoving back her curly hair. "What is it?"

Her aunt looked so upset: there was panic in her eyes and her hair was hanging down with the colorful scarves all loose and tangled.

"Oh, my angel," cried Aunt Ruby, gathering Copper up in a giant hug. "After all these years, when I thought we were so safe! But *they're* here. I thought we were well hidden, and there's never been any sign they were looking for you. . . . Why did I carve that dragon over the door? It was such a giveaway. . . . They were out in the lane at the back. I'm sure, I'm *sure* it was them."

"Who?"

"*Them,*" said Aunt Ruby grimly. "What will we do? Where can we go? And today is your birthday. I never thought . . ."

Copper patted her aunt's back and made soothing noises.

Horrible, horrible, she thought. Aunt Ruby's always so steady. Like a rock. And now? Copper felt as though the floor were collapsing beneath them.

"I shall go to the studio and think," said Aunt Ruby suddenly, drying her eyes and pulling herself together. "It's just been a shock to me. I'm fine. Don't go out of the house," she warned Copper, "and don't open the door to anyone. And don't answer the phone. Don't do *anything* until I've thought. When I've thought, we shall have a plan."

As soon as she had gone, Copper pulled Ralick out from where he had been squashed by Aunt Ruby.

"I think she thought you were a bit of bed," said Copper, pulling his legs straight and twisting his ears upright.

"How could a stuffed toy of my superior quality feel like a bit of bed? I mean, I may be old . . ."

"I know . . ."

"And my ear is loose and my leg joints aren't what they were, but . . . I can still sing!"

And Ralick launched into "Happy Birthday."

Copper smiled and hugged him. "You darling, darling thingy!" she crooned. "Where would I be without you?"

"Cuddling thin air," said Ralick.

"Did you hear what Aunt Ruby said? About these men looking for us?" Copper asked him. "I don't know what she means—were we lost? Why's she so upset?"

"I expect we'll find out," said Ralick, "when Aunt Ruby's ready to tell us."

Since it was long past the time Copper should have set off for school, she dressed in her home clothes and had breakfast on her own. Then she tried to be useful and tidy up, but she couldn't concentrate and sat and knitted row upon row of loose, open stitches instead until her aunt called her into her studio.

Aunt Ruby was sitting at her desk. Piled around her were papers and timetables, notepads and pencils. She looked up at Copper without smiling.

"I'm still thinking," she said to Copper calmly. "A plan is forming. This has been a shock but we will recover." She took Copper's hand and squeezed it tightly. "Most of all— coward that I am—I'm frightened of what you'll find out, about me. . . . You might think I did things wrong. . . . You might be angry with me. But Copper—Copper, I love you as if you were my own dear daughter."

Copper looked out the window. The word *daughter* made her want to cry. She wasn't anyone's daughter.

"You couldn't ever be bad, Aunt Ruby. I love you and I'll always love you, no matter what you've done."

"Maybe," said Aunt Ruby grimly. "Maybe. In the meantime, pack a small bag with plenty of warm clothes. You may be going away."

Copper closed the door softly and went back to Ralick. "I may be going away," she told him.

"Going away?"

"Yes. Aunt Ruby didn't say *we* were going, only *me!*"

"I can feel in my bones that this will be an important day," said Ralick.

"I might believe you if you really had some bones," said Copper.

So Copper packed her bag and waited.

She waited in the kitchen and she waited in her bedroom. She waited in the sitting room. Once she peeped outside into the gloomy gray afternoon and thought she saw a figure lurking by the gate, but perhaps it was just the next-door neighbor. She began to wonder if her aunt was ill. People did suddenly go peculiar, didn't they? After all, *she* hadn't seen these men. Perhaps they didn't even really exist.

Later, Copper took some food in to Aunt Ruby. She couldn't knock because of the tray in her hands, so she called out, "It's me," and went straight in. As she went in, a large bird flew out through the window.

At least, Copper thought it was a bird. . . . She heard the *waffle, waffle* noise of wings flapping and thought she saw a brown feathery body briefly outlined in the window, but she wasn't absolutely sure.

"Oh! A bird!"

"No, no, there wasn't a bird. What an idea. In my *studio?* Copper, you have such an imagination. What sort was it? An eagle?" She laughed. "Come and sit here."

Copper loved her aunt so she sat down and didn't mention the bird again, but there was a feather on the windowsill that hadn't been there before.

"Copper," said her aunt, smiling firmly. "I've made up my mind. It is time for you to leave me. Time for you to go home."

"Go home? But this is my home."

"Your real home is in the Marble Mountains. That's where you come from, where we both come from. Home is where this came from." Slipping her hand into one of the pockets of her apron, she brought out a tiny gold charm.

"This is the last charm, Copper, the tenth and last charm. I suppose you've been hoping a long-lost relative sent it each year, haven't you, and I've let you have your dreams, because—well, I had my reasons, Copper. I had all the charms here and . . ."

"You had them *here!* Nobody sent them?" Copper struggled to make sense of it. "And this is the last? I thought they'd go on forever." She was aware of a cold, empty feeling in her tummy. "If they stop . . . well, then, I might stop."

"There were only ten charms. Maybe it's because this is the last charm that things have started to happen. I don't know. But you won't stop. Dear girl, I think you are just beginning! Look at that golden charm, look at it! Isn't it divine? Nobody ordinary could have made that and nobody ordinary could own it, believe me."

Copper turned the tiny charm over in her hand. "But I don't want things to change," she whispered.

"But all things *do* change," said Aunt Ruby calmly. "Now, Copper, listen. Here is a train ticket to take you to the Marble Mountains. They'll be expecting you."

Copper stared at her aunt. "Who will?"

"Copper, I . . . OH!" Aunt Ruby jumped as something banged outside and voices shouted across the street. "I'm so nervy. . . . Where was I? Take Ralick, of course—he's important. Have you packed warm clothes? Good. The taxi's waiting to take you to the station. Don't get off the train until you reach the mountains. I must stay here and try to put them off the scent. Then later if you ask me . . . if you can forgive me . . . I'll come."

Copper hugged her aunt. "I can't just go! I can't leave school and all my friends and—"

But I can, she thought. I can. I want to. I don't care. *The Marble Mountains.* What do I care about school? Nothing, and I haven't any friends, not really. I shall miss Aunt Ruby, but she'll find me again. And maybe I do have parents, a real family, and maybe I'll stop being all knotted up and tangled inside when I get there. I want to go!

"There's no time to lose. Here, don't forget the bracelet," Aunt Ruby added, pressing it into Copper's hand. "Don't let it out of your sight. It's very, very precious and *they* want it. But it's yours. It was made for you. And, Copper, take this too, this lovely blue wool. I was going to give it to you for your birthday and it *is* your birthday! They'll look after you in the Marble Mountains. Now, you must hurry!"

16

Copper scurried to the door but Aunt Ruby caught her and held her for one last minute.

"If you ever meet a boy called Linden, yes, *Linden,* be nice to him, be kind to him for me. . . . I'll come when you're ready for me. Good-bye!"

4. The Journey

THAT WAS HOW Copper came to be on the train heading for the Marble Mountains, and she was knitting to get herself back together again.

Copper knitted without a pattern, which didn't matter, as she never finished anything. She knitted all the stitches there were, all jumbled up together, pearl, plain, cable, and she could put in loops and bobbles and different colored patterns too.

"Click, click, click," muttered Ralick. "That noise could drive an ordinary cuddly toy crazy."

"Just as well you're not an ordinary cuddly toy then," said Copper. She stared at him. "I've just had an idea, Ralick. How do you fancy wearing a hat?"

"A hat? You mean a blue hat made by you?" asked Ralick, eyeing the wool suspiciously.

"Yes."

"I don't. Especially as it won't be finished."

"No, really, Ralick, this time I'll do it properly. Then I can hide the charm bracelet inside the hem."

"Blue's not my best color," said Ralick.

Copper patted his head. "You'll look as beautiful as ever."

And Copper did it. As the train rocketed through the countryside, she knitted her first complete garment.

"It's the first thing I've ever finished," she whispered, holding it up. "Don't you think that's amazing?" She slipped it onto Ralick's head. "I mean, all the knitting I've done—the gloves with no thumb and the sweaters with no sleeves—and all of a sudden I manage to finish a hat for you."

"Hmm," said Ralick.

"Well, I think it's great. It's an omen."

She took the bracelet out of her bag. It shimmered and glowed in the train lights so brightly that she quickly tucked it under the table.

"It's so bright!" she hissed.

"And you want me to put it round my head? It might interfere with my brain, like electricity."

Copper grinned. "It might make it work better."

"It works very well as it is, thank you."

"It is lovely, isn't it? Aunt Ruby told me I was four years old when she found me because there were four charms on it."

"I know, I know," said Ralick.

"But . . . ," wondered Copper, "but if I was lost, how does Aunt Ruby know where my real home is? And how did she know that having four charms meant I was four years old?

When I try to think back to before Aunt Ruby, I can't. Don't you remember anything?"

"No," said Ralick. "I'm only a cuddly toy."

"But a very special one," she reminded him. "These were the first four charms: a little dog, a heart and two babies that seem to be the same. Then for my fifth birthday I got this lovely bird, then I got the—the mountain! I'm going to the *mountains* now. A coincidence, d'you think? I've never seen a mountain on a charm bracelet before. It must mean something."

"And one of the babies could be you?" suggested Ralick.

"Yes! Why not? Then maybe I've got a sister somewhere? Or a brother? And, Ralick, this dog thing, this could be you!"

"Dog thing? I'm not a dog thing. A pedigree thing, please. Yes. It could be me. Immortalized in gold. Splendid . . . And when you were seven?"

"A coin, a funny one with a tree. I don't know what that could mean. Then a tree on its own and then that lovely miniature pair of knitting needles—well, I do a lot of knitting—and then finally, today's charm, which was this . . . a hammer." Copper made a face.

"Just what every ten-year-old yearns for," said Ralick.

"Well, it is a lovely hammer," said Copper, staring at the tiny object. "Someone must have taken ages to make it. I'm certain each of those charms has a meaning, a special meaning for me."

Copper rolled the ribbed hem of the hat over the bracelet,

then sewed it down. She snuggled the hat down over Ralick's head, pulling his ears through two prepared holes, and tied it under his chin.

"I look like a proper ninny!" growled Ralick, looking at his reflection in the dark of the train window.

"You look as adorable as ever," said Copper brightly. "I'm so proud! The first knitting I've ever finished! It's a real accomplishment!"

"You're right there. You've accomplished making me look like a ninny," said Ralick.

Copper hugged him. "Ralick, I do love you."

The train journey lasted for hours. People got off, but nobody ever got on, and late in the night, Copper found she was the only person left on the train except for the friendly guard. "Last stop coming up in a few minutes," he called cheerily. "Better get your coat on, it's cold out there!"

At last the train wheezed and slithered to a standstill.

"And here we are, the end of the line," said the guard, lifting down Copper's bags. "I hope someone is meeting you, young lady?" he asked her, opening the train door and peering out into the dark.

"Yes," said Copper. "It's home."

"Well, it's a long way from mine," smiled the guard. "Good-bye now!"

Copper stepped outside into a snow-covered landscape. The platform, hedges and trees, station and walls were knee-deep in a thick white crust. The train backed away, screeching and clanking, and suddenly Copper was alone.

Completely alone.

Blackness crept in all around her. The icy cold crawled over her hands and face and tiptoed up her spine, making her shiver and gasp. Her feet grew numb as they sank, with soft squeaks and crunching noises, into the snow.

In front of her was a large, dimly lit sign: END OF THE LINE—MARBLE MOUNTAINS, but apart from that there were no lights, no waiting room, people, cars or anything.

A few large, whirling snowflakes bumped gently against her cheeks and blurred in her eyes.

"Some people would be scared," she said to Ralick in a trembling voice.

"Some people are softies," said Ralick. "Not us."

Suddenly a distant soft howl quivered through the air. Copper yelped and squeezed Ralick. "What was that?"

Then another sound broke the silence, the sound of jingling metal and the muffled clip-clop of horses' hooves growing closer. Then two softly glowing yellow lights pierced the blackness, and Copper saw that they were hung on either side of a large old-fashioned sled. The sled, pulled by two massive horses snorting out clouds of steamy breath, glided round the bushes and stopped in a spray of snow.

"Copper! Copper Beech, is that you?" cried a voice from the sled, and a boy jumped down and ran toward her.

"Who else were you expecting at the end of the line in the dead of night?" said Copper, laughing with relief.

"It *is* you!" cried the boy. "You sound like Copper should sound. I'm Questrid," he added, peering into her eyes intently. "I've come to take you back to Spindle House. Welcome home!"

PART TWO

THE MARBLE MOUNTAINS

5. Spindle House

Questrid wore so many layers of different green and red clothes, he looked like a well-filled veggie sandwich. He had a striped scarf wound round and round his neck, over his chin and up to his ears, and on top of it all was a large hat and at the bottom of it all, big waterproof boots. Beneath his hat, two golden brown eyes gleamed like honey.

"In you get," he said, helping Copper into the sled and covering her with blankets and fur rugs. "Cold? Sorry I was late." Then he jumped in beside her and, flicking the reins at the horses, turned the sled out of the station and into the blackness.

Copper guessed Questrid was about twelve or thirteen, but he was so lanky and half hidden by his clothes, she wasn't sure. He kept looking at her thoughtfully, as if she were a rare, bizarre creature, then grinning as if he found her very amusing.

Copper found it amusing too. She realized she was smiling and that her insides were singing happily.

26

I've never even set eyes on this Questrid before, she thought, but I like him, like he's an old friend. And I've never been in a sled before; never been to the Marble Mountains before, but I love it. I feel as if I've always loved it. It feels just right.

She didn't want to spoil the moment by asking questions, so she snuggled into her seat and watched the broad backs of the two horses rhythmically rising and falling as they cantered down the road, their manes streaming up and down over their gleaming necks.

It was too dark for Copper to see anything other than vague black shapes in the blackness, but it didn't bother Questrid and the horses, they knew their way home. They whooshed over the snow, the sled runners making a hard knife-cutting sound, the horses' hooves pounding.

The freezing air whipped against Copper's cheeks and seemed to seep right into her head and freeze her mind. The noise of the clinking metal on the harness, thundering hooves and the *whoosh, whoosh* of the sled runners lulled her into a mindless trance, so that very soon, much against her wishes, she drifted off to sleep.

She woke just as the sled was slithering to a standstill.

"Spindle House," said Questrid. "Home."

Copper peered out from the blankets and saw there was some sort of a building beside them, lighted windows and two huge carved wooden doors. Looking up into the dark, she could only vaguely make out the rest of the house, but it seemed in her sleepy state to look like a strange spiky tree.

27

Then the doors opened and light streamed out, along with a very big silvery dog that lumbered over to greet her. Copper shrieked and hid behind Questrid.

"It's only Silver," said Questrid, patting the creature's head. "She's gentle as a lamb."

A short woman, smiling so much she could hardly speak, took Copper by the hand and led her gently into the hall.

"Welcome, dear, welcome home," she said. It was too much for Copper: she burst into tears.

"I never cry," she sobbed. "I'm usually brave, it's just that . . ."

"You don't have to say anything. I know. Of course it's too much. And it's late. Come on, my dear, come on with me. I'm Oriole. I'll look after you."

She led Copper up the spiral wooden staircase and helped her into a small bed with stiff, old-fashioned sheets. She tucked her in, muttered more endearments and then went softly away.

Copper lay for some minutes staring into the dark, wondering about it all, then closed her eyes, too exhausted to think. But just before sleep completely overtook her, it seemed that someone crept stealthily into the room and stood beside her, staring at her. . . . But she was so nearly asleep, perhaps it was a dream.

6. THE FIRST DAY

WHEN COPPER WOKE the next morning, she lay very still for a few minutes without opening her eyes, aware that the sheets against her skin were different from the ones at home, that the pillow was fluffier and even that the room smelled different. Then everything that had happened the day before came flooding back.

She was in Spindle House, in the Marble Mountains.

Chirp, chirrup, chip, chip, chirrup.

It was a bird. That's what had woken her. She opened her eyes, squinting at the intense white light, and saw a thrush perched on the back of the chair beside her. The bird was so close that Copper could see its tongue wobbling and its throat vibrating.

Chirrup, chirrup!

Copper sat up slowly. The thrush went on singing and looking at her with its soft brown eyes for a whole minute before it sprang up and flew out the window.

On a tray beside the bed was a cup of hot chocolate and a

warm cinnamon bun, which Copper quickly demolished. Then she lay back against the big pillows. She wanted the moment to last forever.

Her room was the most extraordinary room she'd ever seen.

It was all wooden: the floor, ceiling, walls and all the furniture were made of wood. Her small wooden bed had two short posts at the bottom and two taller ones at the top, and every inch was carved with plants, animals and knobbly faces. The chair was carved with flowers and bees. The large mirror-fronted wardrobe had two trees carved on it with branches interlacing above the doors.

The floorboards creaked gently under her and were warm against her skin despite the sharp cold of the air as she went to peer out the small window.

It was magnificent. She could see for miles and miles, and for miles and miles there was nothing but snow: glistening white and yellow in the sun, purple and violet in the shadows. There were no other houses or buildings in sight, only trees and rocks. In the distance were icy blue peaks of faraway glaciers and mountains. The air was fresh and clean like toothpaste.

"Brilliant," she said.

"It looks very wet and cold to me," said Ralick gloomily. "Can't think what you find so—*gulp!*"

Copper suddenly leaped on him, squeezing him so hard, he choked on his words.

"Shh!" She held her finger to her lips. "Listen. There's someone outside the door."

There was a small shuffling noise and boards creaked, the soft sound of clothes brushing against a wall.

"Someone's spying on us," she hissed, bounding to the door and yanking the handle. But the door latch was stiff; it wouldn't budge. She rattled it angrily. How dare anyone spy on her!

She snatched the door open at last and leaped outside.

The corridor was empty.

"But there was someone there," Copper said furiously. "Spying on us, listening to us."

"Correction, listening to *you*," said Ralick.

"Who could it have been?"

"Perhaps it was a Snow Ogre who fattens up little girls on cinnamon buns and then eats them," said Ralick.

"Ha, ha," said Copper. "Why would anyone spy on me? Let's go and investigate."

She dressed quickly and stepped out into the corridor.

Now Copper saw that it wasn't only her room that was odd—the entire house was very peculiar. Everything was made out of wood and not a single bit of it was straight: the walls curved in and out, the floorboards undulated like frozen waves and above her head, the wooden ceiling arched into a beautiful dome.

She followed the corridor, which was narrow in some places, wide in others, as it curved round onto a circular landing with a large carved cupboard. Two more corridors led off this, as did a spiral staircase going down.

"Isn't it fantastic?" she whispered, staring wide-eyed at it all. "And have you noticed the smell, Ralick? Sweet and warm and honeyish. Let's go down."

The wooden stairs creaked and groaned noisily under her.

"What a racket," growled Ralick.

Copper didn't say anything for a moment, then said shyly, "Yes, but you know, I think they're sort of talking to me."

"Ha! As stairs have a habit of doing!" said Ralick.

"But really, they *are,*" she insisted. "I'm sure, and the handrail too. They're sort of speaking—not words exactly, just voices. I've never touched a handrail like this before. It's soft under my fingers, not soft like cotton, but not solid. . . . It moves. And it smells so gorgeous . . ."

Copper felt more and more excited as she descended the stairs. Everything seemed to her to be so absolutely right. I've missed this, she thought. Then she thought, But how could I? How could I miss something I've never seen?

At the bottom of the stairs Copper paused and looked around. Which way? One door had a picture of a chair carved into it, another door was covered in flowers and on a third there were books.

"Clues," she whispered to Ralick. "Sitting room, garden and library. Ah ha! And that one," she pointed to a door beyond the stairs with fruit, vegetables, cakes and bread carved into it, "that's food, so that's the kitchen, I bet. Good, I'm still starving."

She went to the door, and was just about to go in when she paused, hearing voices talking in hushed tones. She went closer and listened.

"You wouldn't listen to a private conversation, would you?" gasped Ralick.

"No, well, but . . ."

Grr. A low, deep, rumbling growl erupted beside her and she stopped.

"Ralick? Was that you?"

Then something furry pressed against her leg, and glancing down, she saw the vast gray-haired dog from the night before, Silver.

7. ROBIN AND ORIOLE

COPPER JUMPED.

"Of course I wouldn't eavesdrop," she snapped guiltily, and quickly grasping the door handle, she went in.

"Hello!" cried Questrid.

"What the . . . !" gasped Copper, gazing around in amazement. "Birds!"

They were perched on the counter, on the backs of chairs and along the clothesline hanging from the ceiling. They ruffled their feathers, cooed and trilled, and filled the air with the fluttering and shuffling of wings.

"Come in, dear, come in," called Oriole. "Did you sleep well? All this must be *so* strange for you."

Oriole looked just like the little wooden doll with painted brown hair and a tiny wooden chip nose that Copper had once had. She had the same smooth, round face and red cheeks. She wore her long hair plaited down her back and an old-fashioned dress with a long skirt and large white apron. Her dark, soft eyes were just like the thrush's.

"It isn't strange," said Copper, grinning. "It feels very *un*strange and exciting."

"Good. Good. This is my husband, Robin," said Oriole.

Copper shook hands with Robin, who had a very round tummy, rosy cheeks and a ponytail.

"I hope you like birds?" he asked with a twinkle.

"Yes."

"Good, we've twenty-three at the moment," said Robin. "A few more outside. They're all very tame and will help you if you need it."

"What about the dog, is she tame?" asked Copper, pointing at Silver, who seemed glued to her side.

"Oh, Silver. She's a big thing but very gentle. Yes, she's tame."

"What sort of a dog is she?"

"Silver?" Oriole smiled vaguely. "Oh, some sort of crossbreed. She's got all sorts in her, wolfhound, lurcher . . . I suppose you'd call her a mountain dog."

Robin led Copper over to the table.

"Don't be shy," he said. "Come on in and feel at home. This is where you belong." He lifted Copper's hand and examined it closely. "Will you look at that?" he said admiringly. "A Beech's hand if ever I saw one! Those fingers! And you've that lovely copper hair too! You live up to your name, don't you?"

Copper nodded.

Now that she had a chance to look around the kitchen, she saw it was a peculiar room, shaped like a slice of cake with the sharp end cut off. The wider curved wall had windows in it and the narrow end was where the door was. The room was painted yellow and white with a great many green pots and dishes on the shelves. It was warm and sunny, big and welcoming.

"But you're not my parents, are you?" Copper surprised herself by saying suddenly.

Oriole and Robin shook their heads and smiled.

"No, dear. We're not Beeches. We're Partridges, Oriole and Robin Partridge, from down the valley, and we look after Spindle House for your uncle," said Oriole.

"My *uncle!*" Copper squeaked. "Do you mean he was married to Aunt Ruby?"

Robin and Oriole exchanged a look. "No, dear, I don't think so."

"Greenwood—that's your uncle—will explain when he gets back. Now, sit yourself down and have some more breakfast," said Robin.

Copper sat down, but she couldn't help thinking that it was very rude of her uncle not to be there to greet her.

Oriole went on stirring the porridge, humming and singing a wordless song with many la la las and trills and peeping noises. Exactly the same song the thrush had sung to Copper that morning.

Porridge was served in a wooden bowl, but when Copper picked up the wooden spoon to eat, she shrieked and dropped it again. "It moved!"

"Of course it did," said Robin, laughing. "You're from the Wood clan all right."

"It was just settling into your hand, dear," explained Oriole quietly, "so as to be comfortable and friendly. Didn't you notice the chair moving under you too, and perhaps the banister on the stairs?"

"I did," said Copper. "I told Ral . . . I mean, yes, I did feel it move and sort of speak too."

"Just the wood being friendly. I expect it's pleased to have you home too."

Copper squeezed the spoon more firmly and felt it soften and mold itself into her palm until it was a perfect fit. "I love it."

"The house is an old spindle tree, you see. Spindle trees are usually quite small but this one grew to an immensely vast size," Robin explained. "That's why the rooms are such funny shapes. Spindle wood is strong and supple, used for making spindles, of course, though not this one. But you'd know about all that, being a Beech."

"No, I wouldn't," said Copper. "I've just been living with Aunt Ruby."

"Ah, yes," said Robin.

"Never mind," said Oriole, coming over to the table with a bowl of porridge for herself. She put the dish on the table, then carefully turned round three times before sitting on the chair. She saw Copper watching her and smiled.

"It's what Silver does," she said, "and I expect she has a good reason for it, so I do too."

Copper giggled.

"Did your alarm clock go off this morning?" asked Questrid.

"The thrush? Yes," said Copper. "It was lovely."

"Spindle House is still a tree, you see, and we like to share it with the birds. They do all sorts of things in exchange."

Copper looked puzzled.

"Like messages," said Questrid, laughing. "Your aunt Ruby sent us a bird to say you were coming."

"Aunt Ruby? But what about the telephone?"

"Oh, we don't have one of those. The phone lines don't come up into the mountains. Besides, bird-o-gram is a wonderful system."

Copper thought about the feather in her aunt's bedroom. Of course, that explained it. It seemed there was a whole secret world about which Copper knew nothing.

"Aunt Ruby was scared," she told them. "Two men were after me—I saw them at the station."

Oriole looked serious. "Yes. She thought you'd be safer here, and . . . but . . . we can't explain. It's not our story to tell. Wait for your uncle to explain."

She stopped abruptly and stood quite still, listening. Somewhere outside a bell was ringing loudly: *Ding, ding, ding, ding!* it repeated again and again, clear and alarming in the quiet morning. Copper looked at the others.

"What is it?"

But Oriole and Robin and Questrid were already on their feet and running for the door.

"Fire!" they cried. "Fire!"

8. THE ROCKERS

COPPER PICKED UP Ralick, dragged on a big red coat, stuffed her feet into a pair of wool-lined boots she found by the door and followed the others outside.

The air was cold and crisp and took her breath away.

"Can I help?" she asked, hurrying along after them.

"No! Stay there!" Questrid spoke so sharply that Copper sank down on the nearest seat, dejected.

"That's telling you," said Ralick.

They were at the back of the house in a cobbled courtyard. Across the yard were the two sled horses puffing warm clouds of steam over the stable door and stamping their feet. The bell was ringing out the alarm in a small tower on the roof above them.

Copper walked round the yard and was surprised to see a large black-back gull standing on the roof, tugging at the bell rope with its beak.

How clever. I wonder where the fire is.

Soon the others came in under the archway and Robin whistled a signal and the seagull stopped, called out to them, then flew away.

"Is everything all right?" Copper asked.

"Yes, don't worry," said Oriole, going back into the house. "Come back into the warm. We've put out the fire. It was only tiny."

"You'll have to tell her," said Questrid as they trooped back into the kitchen.

"Tell me what?"

"About the Rockers," said Questrid.

"Our neighbors up in the hills who are not very friendly," said Oriole, darting a warning look at Questrid. "The Rockers, we call them. They shot these." She held out three arrows with blackened tips. "These were on fire when they shot them at the house and as you can imagine, with a wooden house we have to be careful."

"But the birds are on guard all day," said Robin, gently lifting a sparrow off his chair. "And they plucked them out of the roof and dropped them into the snow."

"But why do these Rocker people do that? They must hate you."

"The Rockers live in the Rock, up in the mountains. And, yes, they do seem to hate the inhabitants of Spindle House and have for years."

"Why?"

"Now, now," Oriole interrupted, "that's all over and done

with, isn't it? That's just the past, that is. Questrid, are you going to take Copper to look round?"

"Sure," said Questrid. "Come on, Copper. I'll give you a guided tour." He handed her a coat.

"Oh, all right," said Copper, putting it on. "But I would like to know about the Rockers."

"Plenty of time. Now, off you go—and Questrid," Oriole added quietly, "keep your eyes peeled."

"It's freezing out here!" cried Copper, stepping out into the snow.

Questrid grinned. "I'm used to it. There's Thunder and Lightning," he said, indicating the two horses. "Aren't they lovely? I live up above them. I've got my own room and I look after them."

"Don't you want to live in the house?"

"No, I like it with the animals best, and with me not being family and everything . . ."

"I thought . . . isn't Robin your father?"

Questrid laughed. "Of course not! He's from down the valley."

"So?" she said.

"Well, I couldn't be from down the valley. That's all the Partridges and the Peacocks, the Parrots and Woodcocks. Bird clans. I don't look like them, do I?"

Copper shook her head.

"I don't look like anyone, really. Mind you, although you've got the Beech hands, you don't look absolutely Beech."

"How do you know?"

"I know your uncle, don't forget, and there are pictures, portraits. The Beeches are very tall, with red or golden hair and green eyes—yours are nearly black. And they have freckles—you don't. They have long fingers and toes like you, though. They do fantastic things with wood. Do you?"

Copper thought of her attempts at stone carving. Dreadful. Nothing had emerged except a blob. But she had never tried carving wood.

"Come this way," said Questrid. "I want you to see Spindle House properly. You can't see the garden, it's all under snow and there's a lake too, all iced over."

The sky was palest blue with high, thin misty clouds. A weak sunshine made the crusty edges of snow glisten and sparkle. The snow crunched under their feet as if they were treading on eggshells. Copper breathed in the fresh air greedily.

"I love it," she said. "I feel wonderful here."

Questrid smiled. "Of course you do. It's where you belong. Can't cut a twig off a tree then stick it in concrete and expect it to thrive, can you?"

Copper shook her head, although she wasn't sure she understood. Still it was good to be told she belonged, to even begin to feel as if she belonged.

They walked through an archway to the front of the house where the big double doors were. Over them, carved in great detail, was a large, long-tailed dragon.

"That's just like Aunt Ruby's dragon," said Copper. "Did

she live here? She told me she had a dragon when she was little. I can believe it now that I've seen this place."

Questrid smiled. "Was it very boring where you've been living?"

"Very."

The house really was a massive tree. It was brown and tree shaped with very large, thick branches in which small windows were arranged.

Copper ran down to the wall at the end of the garden to get a good look at it.

"I've never seen anything like it!" she cried. "It's the weirdest house in the world, but I think it's great. Oh, look," she added. "Look up there."

Right at the top, at the highest window, a magpie was fluttering, as if it were trying to get inside. It landed on the windowsill, tapped on the glass with its beak and, when the window opened, disappeared inside.

"Did you see that?" Copper squeaked.

"What? I didn't see anything," said Questrid.

"Someone's up there! Someone let the bird inside. Oriole said Uncle Greenwood's out. Who else lives here, Questrid?"

"No one," said Questrid. "I didn't see anything. There are birds all over this place."

"There must be someone up there," said Copper. "Someone opened the window."

But Questrid wasn't interested. He had his eye on Ralick.

"I saw that funny-looking old teddy last night when you

came," he said thoughtfully. "How come you take him every-where?"

"He's not a teddy and he's not funny-looking," snapped Copper, suddenly embarrassed. "He's Ralick."

"*Sorry,*" said Questrid, grinning. "Is there something wrong with his head? I mean, does he have to wear that hat thing?"

"*Hat.* Just a plain hat, not a hat thing. I made it."

"Let's have a look at him," said Questrid. He turned Ralick over and over in his hands and stared into his glass eyes.

"I don't know why, but I feel like I know this ted . . . Ralick," said Questrid, looking confused and worried. "Could I have seen him somewhere, in a book or something? Is he famous?"

"No," said Copper, laughing as she took Ralick back. "I bet he wishes he was, but he's just Ralick."

9. WOOD AND STONE

THEY WALKED RIGHT round Spindle House. At the back, the north side, the ground sloped steeply upward toward the mountains. Dotted over the hillside were clumps of dark trees and large bare rocks that stuck out sharply black against the whiteness of the snow.

"Look up there," said Questrid, "over to the right and you'll see the Rock. That's where the Rockers come from."

Copper strained her eyes, peering into the distance. "I can't see anything."

"It is hard to see," said Questrid. "It's really just a mass of tunnels and caves, built right on top of the mountain with windows at the front. The Rockers are completely isolated up there in their stone fort. If they do venture out, it's only to do evil, like try to set Spindle House on fire. Copper, you're shivering. I *am* sorry. Come up to my room where it's warm."

Copper grinned. "I'm not acclimatized yet."

At the back of the stable, behind the horses, was a ladder

leading up to a long attic room where Questrid slept. There were four tiny windows in the sloping roof and a stove in the corner. There was a wooden bed with a patchwork quilt, a carved chest of drawers and a chair. On a table were some peculiar chunks of wood that seemed to have been hacked at roughly. Copper picked one up.

"What's this?"

Questrid grinned. "Can't you tell?"

"No."

"It's a horse. I carved it. See, four legs and a tail and a head."

Copper made a face. "Don't tell me—you were wearing a blindfold and woolly mittens when you made it."

Questrid shook his head.

"You had one hand tied behind your back?"

Questrid laughed. "No. I just can't carve wood. When I was little, I used to try so hard. I badly wanted to be part of the Wood clan and belong. But I just can't do it."

"So if you're not a Wood, what are you?"

Questrid looked away. "Well . . . ," he began, but Copper interrupted him.

"Who's this?" she said, picking up a framed picture.

"I got it out of a magazine," said Questrid, blushing. "I used to pretend it was my mother. I thought my mother might look like that, I don't know why. There was something about her."

Copper nodded. "I know. I understand."

"I don't know who I am," Questrid told her. "Greenwood

found me years ago, sheltering by a rock in a blizzard. He brought me here and no one ever claimed me, so I stayed. I was about six or seven then. They called me Questrid because Questrid was a famous hunter, and it turned out that I was really good at tracking animals and people, following prints in the snow—you know, that sort of thing."

"So you were a foundling too."

"*Too?* But *you* weren't."

"Yes, I was, I was found by Aunt Ruby," said Copper.

Questrid looked puzzled. "I don't understand. You're a Wood. Everyone knows that. You're not a foundling. I thought you'd just been living somewhere else. Didn't you know you were a Wood?"

"No. I didn't know this place existed until yesterday. Now it seems strange that I've never asked Aunt Ruby more. . . ." She gazed out the window toward the Rock. "I'm going to find out, though," she added. "And I want to know more about the Rockers. Who are they?"

"They're miners and metalworkers, like dwarves of long ago. The Beech family used to trade with them; the Rockers gave them metal and gold that they dug out of the rocks and we gave them wooden things and fruit and vegetables and stuff from the valley. But then there was some terrible row, I think about money, and now there's a sort of war between us. They still mine the rocks, of course, but I don't know what they do with it. People say they keep the Rock all shuttered up and dark. They're our enemies, all the Stone people are. . . ." Questrid's voice trailed off.

"What? Why don't you go on?"

Reluctantly Questrid went across to the bed and pulled something out from under it. He held it up for Copper to see. It was the head of a dog, carved out of gray stone.

"Oh, it's beautiful," cried Copper, stroking the sculpted head. "It's Silver, isn't it? Did you do it?"

Questrid nodded.

"Well, what are you looking so glum about? Aunt Ruby's always making things, always carving things out of stone! You should be proud you can do it. I never could, though I tried—I can't do anything!" She looked up at Questrid and was surprised to see his cheeks blazing red and his eyes shining with unshed tears. "What is it?"

"It's all right for your aunt Ruby—she doesn't live up here, does she? Don't you see what it means? That I might be a Rocker too, a nasty Stone person, like *them*, and I don't want to be!"

"But you couldn't be . . . you're nice."

"And if I was one of them," Questrid went on, "a Rocker, then they might send me back, mightn't they? And I don't ever want to leave here. Never."

A sharp *tap tap* on the window made them both spin round in surprise. A dove had landed on the sloping roof outside and was knocking at the glass with its beak.

Questrid opened the window, glad to have the chance to change the subject, and the bird flew onto his arm.

Coo, coo, it whispered.

"Coo, coo, yourself," said Questrid. "And thank you very

much," he added, slipping the piece of paper out of the tiny wooden holder on the bird's leg. "It's a message from Robin."

"What does it say?"

"That your uncle is ready to see you."

10. Uncle Greenwood

COPPER LOOKED SERIOUS.

"It isn't every day you get to meet a brand-new uncle," she said thoughtfully. "Is he nice?"

"Oh, yes, very nice, but . . ."

"But what?"

"Nothing . . . but he is peculiar."

"So is everyone, I've decided."

Questrid smiled. "Greenwood is very changeable. Sometimes he's gentle and fatherly and kind, and at other times . . . well, he's never unkind, but he's different."

"Same as all grown-ups, then," said Copper.

"Yes, but him more than anyone," said Questrid. "You'll see. He's amazing at woodwork, though. He can make anything."

It was warm and comforting in the kitchen. Oriole was cooking and Robin was cutting up vegetables, and the room was filled with lovely smells.

"Hello, Copper. Did you have a good look round? I hope

you're getting your bearings. Your uncle Greenwood is here now. He's in the Root Room. Take her, will you, Questrid?"

"Root Room? Let me guess," said Copper. "That's downstairs?"

"Correct."

A small door beneath the spiral staircase that Copper had not noticed before was carved with pictures of chisels, planes, hammers and nails.

"A woodwork room!" said Copper.

Questrid nodded and, opening the door, led Copper down a narrow, twisting stairway. It was gloomy, and the air was thick and warm and earthy.

Copper was aware that her heart was thumping like a machine right up in her throat. I hope Uncle Greenwood likes me. Please let him be having one of his kind and gentle days.

They reached the bottom and Copper found herself staring straight into her uncle's unblinking eyes.

"See you later," whispered Questrid, and he slunk quietly back up the stairs.

Uncle Greenwood didn't speak or move, so Copper, breathing steadily, looked around at the strange room. All the time a little voice inside her kept saying, It's an uncle Greenwood, uncle Greenwood, *my* uncle Greenwood.

She was standing on a thick layer of pale wood chips that covered the rock floor. The smell of freshly sawn wood filled the air. Looking up, she could see how the massive roots of the old spindle tree spread out above her head, forming an arch like an ancient chapel ceiling. The roots clung to the walls in a thick, matted net. The walls themselves were hard earth, and in among the roots were little cupboards and shelves, racks and hooks for the woodwork tools.

In the center of the room was a vast worktable and hanging above it, a large, bright light, like a pumpkin.

Behind the table, still staring at Copper, was Uncle Greenwood. He was thin and very tall with red hair that stood straight off his head. He wore glasses on the end of his nose, which was big and knobbly and freckly.

"I'm sorry. I'm sorry," said Uncle Greenwood, shaking his head. "I didn't mean to stare. It gave me such a shock, seeing you like that. You're so like your mother! The image! I never . . ." He came round the table and put his arms round Copper awkwardly, as if he hadn't had much practice at such things. "There, there," he whispered, as if Copper were a baby. "When this aunt Ruby of yours sent word that you were alive," he went on, backing off again, "well, we didn't know whether to believe it, and Robin said you had the hands, but when I see you, there's no doubt, no doubt at all."

"I'm really like my mother?" Copper asked. "How? Which bits?"

A mother!

She felt a buzzing in her head as if a bee were trapped between her ears. "So I wasn't just found, but designed, like everyone else," she said.

"Ah ha, yes, I think I see what you mean. Real parents. Yes, no doubt at all."

"You must think me odd, or stupid," said Copper, "but it's wonderful to have some pieces of my past at last. Because all the time I haven't had the bits to put together, and now . . . well, even just *seeing* you is a great help. But I think it was mean of you to wait so long."

Copper went on. "Why didn't you see me straightaway? Do Oriole and Robin know my mother?" She shook her head in an attempt to get rid of the buzzing noise. "It doesn't seem fair."

She sounded cold and unfriendly and hated herself for it, but she was unnerved. He knew things about her that she didn't know. Even Questrid knew more about Copper than Copper did. She took a big breath and tried to swallow the lump in her throat.

"Quite right," said her uncle, smiling. "It's not fair. It won't happen again."

Copper returned his smile.

"Come and sit," said Uncle Greenwood, clearing off sawdust from a stool. His hands were elegant, narrow with long rootlike fingers. Something melted a little inside Copper and she sat down.

"When I got here, I knew it was my place," said Copper. "I haven't had to knit once, and usually when things are new, and I get all tangled inside, I have to knit. I'm looking for a pattern, you see, and I know that when I find it, I'll be able to knit it all and finish it, and that will be that."

"Good! Wonderful!"

They beamed at each other.

"Now," said Copper, "please explain who Aunt Ruby is and how she found me and where my mother is. Tell me everything. And is there a father? I mean, I know lots of people have babies without fathers around these days, so that doesn't matter or anything, but I want to know. And who were the men at the station trying to get me, and why . . ."

She stopped and grinned up at her new uncle.

"Very, very like your mother!" said Uncle Greenwood, nodding.

"Good," said Copper.

"Where do I start? It all goes back to the Rock."

"The Rock?"

"Yes. They attacked again today, I hear."

"But what about my mother?"

"Well, Copper, this will be hard, but I must tell you if you're going to learn about your past that your mother . . . your mother was one of *them*."

"One of them?" Copper shook her head. "No. She couldn't have been." She squirmed as if ice had just been dropped down her back. "They're the people you all hate. They're all bad, Oriole said so." She suddenly remembered poor Questrid's face when he told her he might belong to the Rock too. "No. Don't say it!"

"It's the truth. But your mother wasn't bad. I promise you could not find a better person than your mother. Of course we, my brother and I, are from the Wood clan. Your father's name was Cedar Beech. Amber was . . ."

"Amber? Was her name Amber?" It seemed extraordinary

that this man should be able to speak her mother's name like that, so easily, so knowingly, when Copper hadn't ever even known it. "Amber," she repeated. "I wish I'd known her name before. Now I can begin to picture her and make a face for her. And Cedar Beech. I like the names. I like having names to put on them."

"Oh, dear," said Uncle Greenwood, "this is all so difficult. I'm not used to children or explaining things."

"You're not doing so badly. Go on," said Copper. "Please."

Uncle Greenwood repositioned some tools on the table, then went on.

"Amber came from the Rock, she was from the Stone clan. Now, the two families had a misunderstanding about a bit of money going a long way back, and things were not good between us, so for a Rock to marry a Wood, oh, very bad. And then there was Granite . . . he's a Rocker." Uncle Greenwood shivered. "He's an evil fellow and he wanted to marry your mother too. So, you can imagine how he felt when Amber ran away with Cedar."

"Angry?" suggested Copper.

"Furious! Incensed! Crazy!" cried Uncle Greenwood. "Granite said he would get Amber back—as if she were a bit of furniture or something. He swore he would. He stopped all trade with us: look, my chisels are old, my hammer is broken, my knives are worn down. We haven't had new metal here for years. Then one day, Granite attacked. He was determined to kill Cedar: it was terrible. Granite had made himself a silver sword—so cleverly made, so beautiful—you should have seen it flashing and slicing through the air. Your father couldn't match that sword, and when Granite pierced him with it, he nearly died. I can see it now, the way Granite held the sword tip at his throat . . . Terrible! Then his men took Amber. Kidnapped her. We couldn't do anything. If we'd have so much as moved a finger to help, I know he would have killed Cedar."

"But you did try to stop him?"

"Of course, of course, but Amber was so frightened that Granite would kill Cedar, she said she'd go back to the Rock if she could take her child with her."

"Her child? Do you mean *me?*"

Uncle Greenwood nodded.

Copper smiled. "Only if she could take me?"

She didn't want to say anything to her new uncle, she could hardly admit it to herself, but all these years she had wondered whether her mother had abandoned her and not wanted her. Now she was hearing the truth, and the truth was that her mother *had* wanted her, had agreed to go with this horrible Granite so long as she could have Copper with her. Another knot seemed to untangle itself in her insides and she sighed.

"Good," she said. "Then what happened?"

"Then we never saw her again. That was it. Of course we tried to get her back, we did everything possible, but she has never been seen since that day. Nor have you. We don't know how you got away from Granite, who this aunt Ruby is or whether Amber is alive or dead."

"And my father? Did he die then?"

"Your father, no . . ." Uncle Greenwood hesitated. "He was a ghost of a man after Amber left. No wife, no child—nothing except a hatred for Granite. So Cedar went away. He left."

"You mean he's still alive? He's out there somewhere? All I have to do is find him?"

Uncle Greenwood looked at her strangely. "I suppose that's all," he said.

11. More Clues

After that, Copper felt so unraveled she had to do some knitting. She sat in the corner of the kitchen in the rocking chair and knitted and knitted and knitted. A tiny wren hopped and flittered round her shoulders.

"Knit, knot, knit, knot," whispered Ralick.

"Shh. I'm thinking."

She knitted the toe of a sock and pulled it out, then the tail of a bird and pulled that out. In a temper she chucked down her needles and took out her crochet hook and began making a circular mat. Round and round sped her needle, bigger and bigger grew the mat.

"You're making me dizzy," said Ralick.

A mother and a father with names and faces, Copper thought wildly. Maybe alive. Maybe waiting for me. Parents, real parents who didn't leave me, but wanted me. She saw her thoughts like a slithering, knotted mass of tangling spaghetti that she couldn't grab hold of quickly enough to unravel and understand. Did Amber knit? Was Cedar kind? Was he alive?

58

Granite, the baddie . . . Greenwood . . . The horrible men up at the Rock . . . relations? So? So what? My mother was one of them and I think poor Questrid is and I'm starting to think dear Aunt Ruby is too.

"Lunch is ready," called Oriole, coming into the room. "Hello, Copper. My goodness, your needle flies!"

The bell rang for lunch and everyone came in and sat down at the big table. They ate vegetable soup from wooden bowls with wooden spoons, and fresh bread and cheese cut with a rather blunt old knife.

Silver was sitting beside Copper's chair, her big eyes following her spoon on its journey to and from Copper's mouth. The dog settled her chin on Copper's knee and sighed.

"I think Silver's hungry," said Copper a little nervously.

"More than ever. She's going to have puppies," Robin told her. "See how swollen her tummy is? They're due in the next few days, I'd say."

Copper stroked the dog's head shyly and gazed into Silver's yellow eyes. What a strange dog she was. She hardly ever barked, and when she did it was more like a howl. Her shaggy fur was silver tipped and both rough and silky to touch.

I would love one of her puppies for my very own, Copper thought.

After the meal, Uncle Greenwood disappeared downstairs to the Root Room again and Robin went out to feed the birds. Questrid went to the horses, leaving only Oriole and Copper in the kitchen.

"I'll help you," said Copper.

"There's really nothing to do," said Oriole.

"There must be. I'll do anything. Isn't there some brass to polish or something?"

"Not in this house!" said Oriole, laughing. "You go and sit in the sitting room now, that's the door with the chairs on it. I'll bring you a drink. Go on."

"But I could help you make the drinks."

"That's all right, off you go."

Puzzled, Copper went.

Am I imagining things, she wondered, or is Oriole eager to get me out of the kitchen?

Copper was three paces down the hall when she remembered Ralick. Heck! She'd hardly spoken to him all day, and now she'd left him behind.

For some reason she didn't want to admit to herself, Copper tiptoed back to the kitchen and peeped in.

Oriole was setting a tray with what appeared to be somebody's lunch. She poured soup into a blue bowl and placed cheese and bread and fruit beside it. Even a mug and a pot of tea.

Who was it for?

Copper watched in astonishment as Oriole put the tray into the dumbwaiter, closed the door and pushed a button to send it upward.

Robin had shown her the dumbwaiter earlier that morning. It was a small lift for carrying food up to the other floors, to save people from having to trudge up and down the narrow spiral stairs.

But who was she feeding? Not Uncle Greenwood in the Root Room; he had just eaten, and anyway the lift only went up . . . so it must be someone *upstairs*.

Copper remembered the bird she had seen going into the window at the very top of the house. Hmm, something funny's going on here, she decided, and I'm going to find out what.

She crept away with only the slightest feeling of guilt, made her way to the door with the carved chairs and sofas on it and found the sitting room.

As she opened the door a delicate smell of sandalwood and lilac wafted out. Copper hesitated, breathing in the scent, then stepped into the room. It was like walking into a garden. The colors were all earthy brown and green, honey and golden. There was the faintest gentle sound, like wind ruffling the leaves on a mild summer's day, and yet the air was still.

Copper chose a large, low chair with a high back and wide arms. It was very comfortable, padded with cushions, and when she leaned back and closed her eyes, the chair began to buzz quietly beneath her and move, like shifting sand on a beach, until it was perfectly comfortable.

Brilliant chair! Copper thought dreamily, and the chair responded, with a stronger buzz, as if the smallest electric current were running through it and into her.

Then the chair began to sway.

A little alarmed, Copper opened her eyes. Nothing was moving, and yet beneath her the chair seemed to bend and sway as if she were high in the branches of a tree, being lulled to sleep by the wind.

She closed her eyes and fell asleep.

Copper had no idea how long she slept in the special chair, but she woke with a start, aware that something had disturbed her.

She looked around. What was it?

The curtains in the alcove were moving. Someone was there! That mysterious snooper again!

She got up very slowly, tiptoed across the room and flung back the curtain.

Nothing. No one. But behind the curtain was a small door, and she was sure that on the other side of the door she could hear the sound of footsteps, hurrying away.

Then Oriole came in with Silver and a tray with a pot of tea, and she didn't know what to say, so she didn't say anything.

"I brought Ralick for you," said Oriole. "You left him in the kitchen."

"Thanks. I take him everywhere usually, but somehow it's not the same here, is it? I mean, this isn't normal."

Copper sat down again, carefully avoiding the sleeping chair.

"Don't you like that chair?" asked Oriole, smiling.

"It sent me to sleep," Copper told her.

"It was made with palm tree wood and still sways in the wind. Here, come and sit in this oak chair. It's a good solid chair and won't play any tricks on you. Your father made it."

"He made things, like Greenwood?"

"Yes. Look, I'm sure you want to see this," said Oriole, pointing to a picture on the wall. "It's a painting of Greenwood and Cedar when they were little."

"But they're identical!" cried Copper. "Identical twins! So I've sort of seen my father already, haven't I? Weird. Did *you* ever know Cedar?"

"No. Robin and I came up here to help only a couple of years ago."

"I wonder if Cedar ever wrote to Greenwood. Where would *you* go after such a thing? I wonder if he ever thinks of me. Or Amber."

"I wonder," said Oriole absentmindedly as she poured the tea.

Copper didn't sit down for long. She jumped up and began looking round the room at the carved mirrors and carved mantelpiece, cupboards and shelves.

"I love all this stuff," she told Oriole. "I've never tried carving wood, only stone, but I think I should start soon. Aunt Ruby was so good at sculpting things—you've no idea. But I was hopeless. Now I know why. I love knowing why. You see, my life is like a bit of knitting in a way, a bit of knitting that was started but not finished. No, I know, started and then done wrong, dropped stitches and things, and then left. I've got to get myself finished somehow."

Silver padded into the room and came to stand beside her, rubbing against her legs, and together they stared out the window at the fading light.

"Draw the curtains, Copper," said Oriole. "It keeps in the warmth and it's gloomy out there."

Copper tugged and pulled at the long, heavy curtains. "They're jammed." She yanked them hard. Something small and shining dropped down beside her.

It was a tiny gold charm, just like the ones on her secret charm bracelet.

Silver growled quietly.

"What is it?" called Oriole.

"It's a little gold tree charm," said Copper, taking it over to show her. "But it's not lovely, not like the ones I've got . . . I mean, *seen*." Her heart raced, realizing she'd nearly told about her bracelet. Aunt Ruby had said to keep it secret and she must. "There's nothing charming about this charm—look."

It was a tiny fir tree, beautifully made with every pine needle clear, but the tree was bent over, cut almost in half by a long ax thrust into its side.

The message was plain.

"Now, how on earth did that thing get up there?" said Oriole. "D'you think someone threw it there? It's certainly not very nice."

"It's horrid. Who made it?" whispered Copper in a quivering voice. Because surely, she thought, surely whoever made it made my lovely charms too. "Do you know who made it?" she asked again.

"Why, of course," said Oriole. "I'd recognize that style of metalwork anywhere. That charm was made by *Granite*."

12. SLEDDING

THE NEXT MORNING, Copper was awakened by birdsong again. This time it was a fat robin. Copper lay quietly, watching him, remembering everything that had happened yesterday. The sense of excitement, of things yet to come, still absorbed her, and she couldn't help grinning to herself.

"What's that racket?" said Ralick.

"Just the robin," said Copper. "And he's got a message for us." She gently removed the tiny roll of paper from a container on the bird's leg.

Good morning! Breakfast is ready.

The robin flew away and Copper flew out of bed.

"Questrid said he'd take me sledding today," she told Ralick, propping him up on the pillows. "I've never gone sledding before. I'd better not take you, though, it's so cold out there."

"Cold? Bah!" said Ralick. "You're bored with me. You like Questrid better than me."

"Silly creature. I love you, but sledding really isn't suitable for . . . for a . . ."

"Go on, say it. A *cuddly toy!* That's all you think of me now, isn't it?"

"But think, if you fell into the snow you'd get wet and your fur is . . . a bit worn and it's so cold and then there's the bracelet. We mustn't lose that."

"Huh, so I'll stay at home all on my own—maybe I'll take up knotting. You've almost stopped doing that too."

"Knitting," said Copper. "I know I have. I don't feel the need at the moment."

"Bah!" said Ralick again.

Despite Ralick's complaints, Copper left him snug and cozy in the kitchen.

Outside the air was gray and very still and heavy as if clogged with snow just hanging in it and waiting to fall. Copper pulled her hat firmly down over her ears, thrust her hands deep into the pockets of her big, borrowed coat and walked over to the stables.

Silver bounded out from her warm bed beside the horses to greet her.

"Good girl!" said Copper, stroking her luscious fur. "You stay here in the warmth and don't catch cold. You must look after yourself and your puppies."

"Hello," said Questrid. "Here's your sled."

"It's beautiful!" said Copper, gazing at it. It was an old-fashioned design, with curved runners trimmed with a silver metal. There were leather reins attached to the front that swiveled from side to side, and the seat was padded with fur.

"Who made it?"

"I don't know," said Questrid, "but I'm sure it was a Beech. My sled is the same. They're both really fast and well balanced. You'll love riding them."

They pulled the sleds across the yard and headed up the hill.

"Did you find out anything new yesterday?" Questrid asked Copper.

"I told you everything," Copper said. It was easier to talk to Questrid than anyone else. "And now all I can think about is going to look for my mother and father. I wrote to Aunt Ruby this morning, a long letter telling her everything too. I do miss her."

Copper had given the letter to Oriole, who promised to send it on.

"Of course you must miss her. . . . Can you manage that sled? Come on. We'll go up to those pine trees, there," said Questrid, pointing up the steep hill. "Then we can zoom down and whiz straight into the courtyard—right through the arch—without stopping. It's fantastic!"

At last they reached the trees, and dusting the snow off a fallen log, they sat down, panting heavily.

"Now, take a look at that," said Questrid, spreading out his arms at the scene in front of them.

They could see for miles.

Below, Spindle House was dark against the snow. The red

roofs balanced like pointed hats on its branches were the only specks of color. Smoke, trailing out of a chimney at the back, lay draped over the wall like a wet scarf. It was like looking at a toy house, and there was Silver in the yard, a tiny toy dog.

It was very quiet and still. The only sound was the wind gently teasing the pine trees and occasionally the softest *plop* as snow dropped from their branches.

Then Copper heard something else.

Behind the normal earthy noises was a creeping noise, a slithering and sneaky noise. Something or someone was creeping up on her . . . again! But this time the hairs on the back of Copper's neck prickled and she felt really scared. This was different. This was *menacing*.

Her fingers tightened their grip on the fallen tree beneath her.

Copper looked at Questrid. Yes, he'd heard it too. His eyes were as round as saucers. They stared at each other, straining to hear the tiny unnatural sounds: soft slithering of snow, bodies brushing against trees, squelching, crunching snow beneath feet.

Whatever it was, it was getting closer and closer. . . .

Suddenly: "Yahoo! Yahoo! There she is!" a voice called, and six small men stormed out from the cover of the trees and came running straight at them, whirling long pointed swords above their heads and yelling.

"*Rockers!*" cried Questrid, leaping up. "Quick! Get on your sled!"

Rockers? "Two of them were at the station!" cried Copper.

"Come on!" yelled Questrid, ignoring her. He yanked the sleds round, but his foot caught in the reins and he tripped and fell, sending the two sleds across each other, runners jammed and stuck together.

Copper screamed.

The men were coming at them like a flock of angry crows. They were nearly on top of them. She could hear the whir of their swords through the air, see their shining black eyes locked onto her.

Questrid hauled himself up and the two of them pulled at the sleds, tugging them apart. Then suddenly hers was free, and she spun it round to point downhill.

"Hurry, hurry. Get on!" cried Questrid.

Copper threw herself onto the sled just as a man with a black woolly hat and a straggly black beard reached them, grabbing at her, snatching at her clothes.

"GO! GO!" screamed Questrid. He gave the sled a massive push and heaved his shoulder against her.

The sled went.

It shot off with a whoosh like a rocket, swerved as Copper yanked it straight, then went racing, straight as an arrow down toward Spindle House.

Behind her, there were shouts and cries of anger, but Copper didn't dare look back. Was Questrid all right? If she turned she knew she'd fall off. She was too scared to do anything except hold on. What if they were right behind her, reaching and grabbing at her collar?

Hunched down, she urged the sled on faster and faster, and soon there was only the sharp sound of its runners cutting through the icy snow and the cold wind singing in her ears.

Seconds later, the sled slid under the archway and into the courtyard, just like Questrid said it would.

Home.

Copper glided to a standstill and slipped onto the ground. Silver bounded over to her, licking her face, pushing her wet nose against Copper's cold cheek.

Copper wrapped her arms round the dog. "I'm all right."

Before Copper could even scramble to her feet, she saw Questrid's sled heading down the hill, and a second later it came zooming into the courtyard like a bullet.

"Look out!" cried Questrid, swerving round Silver and Copper. "Watch it!" He tumbled off, landing upside down in a pile of snow. "Phew!" he said, dusting himself off. He was grinning from ear to ear. "That was fun, wasn't it?"

"Fun?" cried Copper. "It was scary, more like. They were trying to get me, or didn't you notice?"

"I know, I know," said Questrid. "Sorry. I suppose I'm used to Rockers. Are you all right? Don't look so worried, you're safe now. Come on, I'll take you in and Oriole will look after you."

Copper was trembling as Oriole and Questrid settled her into a chair by the stove.

"It was the way they pointed at me," said Copper. "The way they glared so fiercely at me."

Copper picked up her needles and started: *click, clack, click.*

"Just like old times," whispered Ralick.

"Those Rockers! What a nerve," said Oriole. "They're getting more and more daring. It's Granite, playing at king up there, making them do this."

"She's right about them being after her," said Questrid, sitting down by the fire. "They yelled, 'It's her!' and ran for her like she was important or something."

Copper went on knitting.

"But why me?" she said. Knit one, pearl one, knit one, pearl one: her knitting needles skipped along. "Why me?"

Robin didn't make any comment. Copper had noticed that when she'd finished telling them what had happened, he had quickly scribbled something on a scrap of paper, picked up a blackbird and went outside with it.

He was sending a message, but to whom?

"Yes, why do the Rockers want Copper?" said Questrid.

"I'd never have let you go sledding if I'd thought they'd attack you like that," said Oriole. "I thought you'd be safe with us around, but you're not. No more than you were with your aunt Ruby. But you're all right now."

"Oh, yes," said Copper. "I feel very safe here. They'd never try to get me in here, would they? And I've been thinking about all the things that Uncle Greenwood told me yesterday, about my mother, because I'm sure she's still there, up at the Rock. I'm sure she's not dead."

"Oh, Copper," said Oriole. "Don't get your hopes up, please don't."

"You need to see the place to understand," said Robin,

coming back in at that moment. "It's impossible to get in. Solid rock. They tried, I know they did."

"So you don't think she's in there?"

"No," said Oriole, putting her arm round her. "I'm sorry to say that I don't. I think if she were still there, Granite wouldn't still be fighting us. He'd have given up and settled down with his precious treasure because he would have gotten what he wanted, which was *her*. No, dear, I'm afraid she must be dead or have run away."

"But you don't *know?*"

"No, not absolutely for certain."

Copper went back to her knitting.

They don't know for certain. Well, I shall find out for certain, and if she is alive in there . . . I shall find her.

13. Looking for the Room at the Top of the House

Silver was missing.

"It's not like her at all," Oriole fretted the next morning. "She had her dinner last night as usual and she went out to the stables as usual, but now there's no sign of her. What if she's gone and had her pups somewhere? Or she's hurt?"

"We'll go and search for her later," said Robin. "We've got to go to the station to pick up some provisions this morning," he told Copper. "You and Questrid mustn't leave the house," he added. "It isn't safe after what the Rockers tried yesterday."

"Silver should be on guard," said Oriole worriedly. "Uncle Greenwood's in the Root Room, but he's working on something intricate and I don't think he'd notice if the place exploded."

"We won't be long," said Robin. "Don't worry."

When they had gone, Copper sat at the big kitchen table and wrote to Aunt Ruby again.

Dear Aunt Ruby,

Did you send me away because of the Rockers trying to get me? Well, they tried to catch me here too, but don't worry, I am too fast. Of course I forgive you for everything, but I haven't found anything to forgive you for yet. I wish I knew how you found me. Did you rescue me from Granite? Did you know my parents? Are you really one of those people, those Stone people? I still love you even if you are, because Uncle Greenwood told me that my mother was one so they must be all right. Robin is sending this with one of his birds. Do write back. I miss you and think about you often.

Lots of love, Copper

P.S. I have not met anyone called Linden.

Then, because she hadn't much else to do, she began thinking about the mysterious person she was sure lived at the top of the house, and by the time Questrid came in to get something to eat, she had hatched a plan.

"Questrid, I want you to help me. I think there's someone else living here, secretly."

Questrid looked puzzled.

"Oh, Questrid, haven't you *ever* thought there might be? Think! Who lives up in that tiny room at the top of the tree? Who does Oriole send food up to in the dumbwaiter?"

"I don't know."

"You're very nice but you have no imagination, Questrid. Yesterday, after the Rockers attacked, I'm sure Robin told someone about it. But who?"

"I don't know," said Questrid, helping himself to a slice of cake and sitting down by the fire. "But if Oriole and Robin wanted us to know, they'd tell us."

"Really, Questrid, aren't you interested? Here's a mystery and we need to solve it."

"Do we?"

"Yes. I want us to go up there. Now."

Questrid choked and spat out some crumbs.

"But . . ."

"Come on."

The house was strangely quiet. Even the floorboards were not squeaking and creaking in their normal friendly way today. Copper fancied it was because they were cross with her for spying.

"But I have to," she told them.

"Have to what?" said Questrid. "Or are you talking to Ralick again?"

Copper laughed. "To the stairs, actually."

They crept up the spiral staircase very slowly and onto the circular landing where three long windows, set between the three corridors, let in the sunlight. There was a big chest, a chair and a cupboard.

"Now where?" asked Questrid. "I never come upstairs."

"It can only be up," said Copper, "so we need to find another staircase."

They tiptoed along the first narrow corridor.

"But this is just one of the branches," said Questrid. "It can't go anywhere."

He was right. It got smaller and smaller toward the end, until it was nothing at all. There were two doors on one side, but when they opened them cautiously, there were only empty rooms. They went back to the landing.

"That way is my bedroom," said Copper, "and there's a tiny bathroom, that's all. Let's try the third corridor."

"There can't be stairs there either," said Questrid.

Again he was right. There were just three tiny bedrooms and another bathroom along the third corridor.

No stairs.

Copper and Questrid went back to the landing.

They opened the oak chest but it was full of blankets. The large cupboard with elaborate carvings of deer and mountains was full of clothes. The chair was just a chair.

There were no trapdoors in the ceiling or mysterious cracks in the walls. There was absolutely no way to get into the room at the top of the house.

"You and your funny ideas," said Questrid, grinning. "Now, I'd better go and feed the horses. Don't do anything else crazy while I'm out, and don't leave the house!" He clattered back downstairs.

Copper went back to the kitchen and flopped into her chair.

"What shall I do?"

"Oh, you're talking to me again, are you?" said Ralick. "I thought you'd forgotten me."

"As if I could."

"Anyway, what's the problem?"

"I couldn't find the hidden room and I'm worried about Silver. I'm worried about Aunt Ruby being all alone. I'm worried because I've got an uncle and he's my real uncle but I don't love him like I do Aunt Ruby. I'm worried because the Rockers want to get me but no one knows why. I'm worried because I've got a real mother and a father. My mother may even be up in the mountains living in that horrid Rock place. My father may be there too. So much to worry about!"

"I'll tell you something," said Ralick. "You haven't done so much knotting recently, so you aren't feeling too undone even if you are worried."

"Now, that is true," said Copper brightly. "Ever since I got on that train, I've been feeling more and more together. It's like when you're knitting and you get to the bit where you can start casting off stitches for the armhole. You start shaping it, making fewer stitches, and knitting gets easier and you can see the end of the thing. Well, that's how I feel."

"Huh," said Ralick. "Trouble is, you've never in your life finished anything except this appalling hat, which I hate wearing. I think there's something wrong with it. Once in a while it gets tighter and hotter and more and more tingly. Sometimes I think the gold inside is burning me up."

"You've got a strange imagination."

"I don't have any imagination. I'm just a figment of *your* imagination. But the bracelet is hot."

Copper giggled. "That reminds me. I forgot to show this to you, Ralick. See, it's another gold charm. It fell off the top of the curtains when I drew them."

"What a peculiar place to keep a gold charm."

"I can't imagine how it got up there," Copper agreed. "It looks just like mine but it's *evil,* isn't it? So it couldn't really be like mine, could it?"

"No. Your charms are bursting with nice feelings . . . though since we got up here in the mountains they've changed or the bracelet has changed. It seems to be buzzing and—"

"We're back!" Oriole appeared carrying boxes of food, and Copper helped her put them on the table and began unpacking them.

"I'm glad to see you, Copper. Goodness me, I was so worried, but of course you're all right. Is Silver back yet? She's always there to meet the sled."

"There's no sign of her," said Copper.

"Dogs do sometimes go off to hide to have their pups," said Oriole. "They don't always choose the best places either."

"We'll organize a proper search for her this afternoon," said Robin. "Questrid will find her. You know how good he is at tracking."

"Yes. I hope you're right. Ring the bell for Uncle Greenwood to come up for lunch, will you, Copper?" said Oriole. "We'd better eat quickly. Silver has never disappeared like this before."

14. Copper Investigates the Dumbwaiter

LATER THAT AFTERNOON, Copper was alone again—except for the birds and Ralick.

Sitting in the kitchen, she found her eyes drawn to the dumbwaiter again and again. Who did it carry food to? Where did it go?

"Why not find out?" said Ralick. "No one will know."

Copper sidled over to the dumbwaiter and quickly, guiltily, pressed the button.

The machine hummed into life with a distant rumble and soon the lift appeared and shuddered to a halt. Copper dragged a chair across to it and climbed in. By bending her knees up and squashing her head down, she could just squeeze in. Then she reached round and pressed the *up* button.

Immediately, with a jerk and a shudder, the lift began moving upward into the dark.

Dark! I never thought it would be dark, she worried, as the lift inched its way up into the stuffy woodiness. This is a bad idea, this is a silly thing to do. What if it gets stuck? What if it drops to the ground under my weight?

The ropes whined and the lift rumbled and squeaked.

Where's it going? What's up there? Why do I do these things, and where's Ralick when I need him?

At last a chink of light appeared, then more, and seconds later the lift shuddered to a halt. It had stopped in the middle of a round room with small windows facing out in all directions: the top of the house—at last!

A pair of pigeons cooed and trilled from a shelf and stared down at her with interest. There were chairs and a table, and the curved walls were lined with books.

Gingerly, Copper eased herself out of the dumbwaiter.

Can't see anyone, she thought, but there's Oriole's tray and the food's gone.

Copper crept round. Behind the lift, on the other side of the room, she found a fixed wooden ladder going up through a hole in the ceiling to the floor above.

"Okay, here goes," she said.

She climbed the ladder slowly, her heart pounding in her ribs, her breathing fast and hard. Just before she poked her head out through the hole, she called out, "Hello! Ready or not, here I come!" and pushed her way into the room above.

She couldn't believe what she saw . . .

There were two of them. TWO Uncle Greenwoods!

15. Copper Runs Away

THE MEN HURRIED over to Copper as she scrambled through
the hole in the floor.

"Hey!" she cried as she was scooped up in some long arms
and hugged tightly. "Hey!"

"Copper, my dear," said the owner of the arms. *"Copper."*

Copper angrily wriggled free and stepped back. "How
dare you!" she heard herself say. She stared up at the two
identical faces until they began to swim and skid before
her eyes.

"I think you should explain," she muttered weakly. "I have
this dreadful feeling that one of you is my father, and I think
I'm going to faint."

Before she hit the floor, the uncle Greenwood who had
hugged her caught her and lifted her gently onto a sofa.

"There, there," he said. "You're right, Copper. I am your father. I'm Cedar."

"But you can't be, you're dead, or disappeared and went
away. What are you doing here?" And as she spoke, she knew

81

the answer. "You *couldn't* have been hiding here all the time." She gulped. "You *couldn't* have, but you have, haven't you? It was you spying on me, wasn't it? And it was *you* that Robin sent the message to last night."

"Let me explain," said Cedar.

"You can try," said Copper, sitting up and looking at him grimly, "but it's not going to be easy."

"No, it isn't," he agreed. "But I'll try. Copper, it's so wonderful to see you. . . . Just to know you're alive, after all these years is so, so *incredible.* I wish I could explain how it feels. How am I ever going to make you understand?

"I'll go back to when Granite wounded me in that fight, all those years ago," said Cedar. "He swore he would kill me if he saw me again. And he meant it. If he ever knew I was alive, I'd be dead—if you see what I mean. So I had to hide. That's why I'm hiding now." He was staring at Copper anxiously, but she wasn't going to help him. "Greenwood and I look so similar," he went on, "we devised this plan: one day I come out and do all the things Greenwood would do, and the next, Greenwood comes out and does them. One of us is Greenwood all the time."

"That's crazy," said Copper. "Mad. But now I see why Questrid thought you were so odd: different people on different days."

"It was all we could think of. Without Amber . . . without you . . . I didn't know what to do."

"Did Aunt Ruby know? No, she would never be so cruel." Copper stared at Cedar. "I can't believe it. I've dreamed about having a real father and a real mother but not one like this. Not one who hides from me."

"Copper, don't say that. You must realize that the letter from Aunt Ruby was the first we ever knew about you being alive. Before that I had always assumed you were dead, like Amber."

"And when you *did* know I was alive," said Copper, "why didn't you come and see me? How could you stay up here when I was down there? How could you go on hiding when those Rockers nearly got me? And everyone lied to me. Everyone! How could they?"

"I did come and see you. I watched you . . . ," he began, but Copper got up from the sofa and began backing away from him.

"Don't touch me," she said as Cedar reached out to her. "I can't stay with you. You're not my father. I want Aunt Ruby."

She turned and ran.

She fled down the ladder and burst through the first door she saw, completely forgetting about the dumbwaiter.

She found herself racing down a tiny spiral staircase. It was only when she got to the bottom and found a rack of coats blocking her way that she wondered where she was. She plunged on through the coats, pushing them aside, until seconds later, her fingers touched a handle and pushed it. A door swung out in front of her.

She had opened the doors from the inside of the cupboard on the landing, and now she was standing at the top of the stairs.

So *that* was where the stairs were hidden! But she couldn't stop to think. She was escaping, running away.

Don't cry, she told herself. Don't cry. She knew she would if she set eyes on Robin or Oriole or even Questrid's silly grinning face, but they were out looking for Silver and the kitchen was empty, so she rushed in and grabbed Ralick.

"Ralick," she said, picking him up and kissing him. "This is all so awful."

"Being squashed and kissed, you mean?"

"No, no, finding a father."

The sound of footsteps clattering down the stairs spurred her on. She stuffed Ralick up her sweater, pulled on her coat, hat and boots and ran out into the snow.

Cold, cold air splashed against her hot cheeks like iced water, and Copper staggered back as if she'd been hit, but she put her chin down and stormed off, plowing through the newly fallen snow.

"I'm never going back, never!"

The sky was deep purple and snow was falling—massive soft flakes like soapsuds that caught in her eyelashes and melted on her lips.

"I'll never forgive Cedar," she hissed to Ralick as she stamped under the arch and into the garden.

"You will," his muffled voice came back from deep inside her coat. "He's your father."

"But how could he do that? How could he hide from everyone? Why didn't he come and see me?"

"He did. He watched you, you know he did, he was watching everything that was happening."

"He should have come to meet me," said Copper. "To talk to me."

"I expect it's very hard to meet a girl who's your daughter and you haven't seen her since she was four years old and you've been stuck in a treehouse all those years watching out for mad Stone people."

Despite herself Copper giggled. "But not impossible. He should have come to see me. He should have."

Copper kicked against the snow. It was falling fast, the flakes black in the dark sky, and it was getting harder to see.

"It's not the way I would have done things," she said. "I would have come straight down and hugged me and, and just filled in all the gaps and the time we've missed."

"But he's not you," said Ralick. "He does things his way, and even if you don't like it much, you'll have to accept it. He is your father."

"I know. Just not quite the father I'd planned on having. Other people have time to get to know their fathers. They learn to love them over years and years. The father I'd imagined for myself was so different. . . ."

"What was he like?"

"Oh, he was more handsome—now that I think of it, he looked very much like Action Man. And he carried me about when I was a baby and built me a dollhouse. And he held my hand as we walked through the park. I suppose that's what all orphans imagine. . . ."

"This one might do those things."

"He might. If there was a park and if I'd let him hold my hand. . . . I'll have to go back, I suppose," she said more calmly. "But I don't know what I'm going to say to him. I wish I'd never come—but I love it here. . . . Oh, dear . . ."

Then she stopped.

"Look. Look, Ralick, it's Silver!"

Silver was standing beside a small gate that led out of the garden. She looked like a dirty smudge against the snow, almost a shadow, hardly there at all.

"Silver?"

Silver heard her, her ears pricked up, but then she shrank back, as if she didn't want to come.

"I'll have to go and get her," said Copper. "I wonder what's happened." She trudged across the snow. "Here, Silver! Here!"

But as she got nearer, the dog backed farther away and slunk back deeper into the shadow of the gateway.

Something was very wrong.

Copper glanced back at Spindle House; it was blurred by the snow and looked dim and unreal.

"Maybe it was just a dream, Ralick," she said. "I haven't really got a father and an uncle at all. Spindle House doesn't exist. See how it's disappearing in the snow? If I turn my back on it, it'll go forever."

"Well, don't then," growled Ralick.

"But I've got to get Silver. I mustn't lose the house. I'm scared."

She took three steps backward, watching the house, defying it to vanish in the swirling snow.

"Silver!" she called. "Silver!"

But even her voice was being sucked away. If I'm not careful, there'll be no house, no dog and no me, she thought.

Suddenly, Silver stepped out of the shadows and it was dreadful. Copper staggered backward and gasped, as shocked as if a snowball had hit her full in the face.

Because Silver wasn't Silver anymore. This dog had eyes that blazed yellow and fiery. Her fur was rough and ragged. Her lips curled back in a growl, showing pointed, dangerous teeth. She angled her nose up to the sky and howled: a terrible noise, a nightmare noise.

"She's not a dog. Dogs don't do that," whispered Copper. "Oh, Ralick, she's a . . . *wolf.*"

The word dropped out of Copper's mouth like a stone. *"Wolf!"*

As she spoke, as if on cue, the alarm bell on the roof of the stables suddenly began ringing its warning. Copper turned and ran, crashing with such force into the men who had crept up behind her that she toppled backward.

There were four men with swords and rope. They were on top of her immediately, clamping her hands to her sides, covering her mouth with a foul leather glove and tying her hands together. Copper tried to scream, but only choked. She struggled, kicking wildly, but within seconds she was being bundled onto a sled.

Silver? Where are you, Silver? Why isn't she helping me?

thought Copper. Why isn't she attacking the men? Has she gone for Questrid and Robin?

The men took up the ropes and pulled the sled swiftly out through the garden.

Copper twisted her head from side to side. Silver was there, with *them* . . . why? Then Copper knew. A coldness, heavier and harder than any she'd ever felt before, clogged her heart.

Silver had led the Rockers to her.

Copper felt the hot tears on her face and could do nothing to wipe them away, but nobody saw them as the strange group plodded upward, toward the Rock.

Part Three

Inside the Rock

16. Granite

THE SLED BUMPED and slithered over the uneven surface, and Copper bumped and slithered uncomfortably with it.

She felt the incline of the hill underneath her, but that was the only way she knew they were moving upward. In the yellow glow of their torches, she could only just see the outline of the four men pulling the sled in front of her, and occasionally she caught sight of Silver.

Something awful had happened to make Silver do this. Something terrible.

Bang! Jolt! Thump! The sled crashed over stones and bumped over the snow. "I wish I could move my arms, Ralick," whispered Copper. "They're tied so tightly. I'm glad you're here."

"I'm not," hissed Ralick.

"You are really," said Copper. "You know you are."

"Hmm."

At last they came to the Rock. It loomed thirty or forty

meters up, a sheer cliff of marble and stone, gray and glistening and cold. Deep windows, shuttered and barred, were set into the stone. A great wooden door with huge metal hinges and iron studs on it stood at the top of a flight of black steps. The men hammered on the door and tugged at the iron bellpull until the door was dragged open. Copper was hauled inside, the metal sled runners screeching and scraping over the stone floor.

They untied her and yanked her off the sled. "Get up."

"Come with me," said one of the men. He had long black hair and a black beard that curled around his chest. His eyes glinted as he pointed down a corridor. "That way!"

Copper stared at him. Should she? Or should she run?

"Just do what they say," whispered Ralick. "We're outnumbered. By lots."

So she did.

She shuffled along beside the Rocker, hugging her coat round her. The air was freezing, even colder and damper than outside.

The man led her down a passageway with polished stone walls. The marble floor was slippery and cold, and their feet made a quiet flapping noise as they hurried along as if they were large aquatic animals.

Some miserable candles flickered in lanterns on the walls, but most of the light came from an eerie green vapor floating near the ceiling. It gave everything and everyone a sickly green tinge, as if they were ill or living under water.

What a horrible place to live, thought Copper, and immediately a picture of the warm and beautifully scented rooms
at Spindle House sprang into her mind. She felt a pang of
sorrow. Would she see it again? Ever?

I could never live here, she thought. Never stay in this
terrible stone place. No wonder the Rockers are so bad
tempered and rude.

Every single window was crisscrossed with solid bars and
shuttered, though the shutters themselves were rotten with
sagging hinges, which, Copper guessed, would fall apart if
touched. She remembered that trading wood for metal and
metal for wood had stopped between the families. That
explained a lot.

Copper was taken up a wide stone staircase and locked
into a bare room with nothing in it except a narrow, hard iron
bed with no mattress.

"This is nice," said Copper, sitting down on the bed and
taking Ralick out from her coat.

"Five-star apartment," Ralick agreed. "Thanks for bringing
me along, Copper."

"My pleasure."

They grinned at each other.

"Any chance of me getting rid of this hat?" Ralick added.
"It's worse than ever under here: it seems to be buzzing and
burning. My stuffing's being squished."

"Shh!" Copper hissed. "I know it's not your favorite head-
gear, but you must. Our precious *you know what* is in there,
and I've just realized—I'm so stupid—I bet it's not *me* they

want at all: it's the bracelet and the gold charms they're looking for. Aunt Ruby told me they wanted it, but of course *then* I didn't know it was the Rockers who were after me."

"You should have left me at home then," said Ralick.

"I would have if I'd known we were going to be kidnapped. It's all Silver's fault—Silver the wolf."

"Are you quite sure about that?" said Ralick.

"Why?"

"Well, I remember you saying, back home at Aunt Ruby's, that wolves were very loyal animals and that you would like one as a pet."

"Oh, yes, I did. . . . But Silver seems to be loyal to the wrong person. Loyal to the Stone people."

"That's how it looks," said Ralick.

They sat and stared at the locked door. The hours passed very slowly.

Copper found a crochet hook and the rest of the birthday knitting wool in her coat pocket, so she began to crochet a fancy dressing-table mat. Then she pulled it out and went to sleep.

She woke when the door was pushed roughly and noisily open and two Rockers came in. They were well covered with black, gray and brown clothes, woolly hats and big fur-lined boots.

"At last," said Copper. "You can't keep me locked up like this. It's against the law. My friends will be coming to find me and you'll . . ."

"Be quiet! You don't know anything."

"Hush, Grit," said the other man. "Granite wants you, young lady."

"Granite?" Copper's heart nearly failed her. She fixed a frozen smile on her face. "Ah, *Granite,*" she said, trying to look calm. "Of course."

She got up slowly and followed the men as they led her down a green-tinged corridor to a large metal door. Grit slid it back and pushed her forward.

"Go in."

In front of her another metal door opened, spilling out a brilliant light like golden syrup on fire. The doors slid shut behind her.

Copper held up her hand to shield her eyes as she went in.

It was extraordinary. Hanging from the ceiling were five large chandeliers with red candles burning in them. On the walls were more candles and in the center of the room, a vast pile of gold and precious stones, which shimmered and glistened. Everywhere was light and brilliance.

Something moved in the shadows and Copper turned quickly.

"Ah ha! So this is it. This little stick is Copper Beech, is it?"

It was an unpleasant voice, rattling, like gravel skittering downhill.

Granite was broad, with powerful shoulders, but his body was permanently bent over as if he'd been kicked in the stomach and badly winded. He had long gray hair and his skin was pitted with black dust. His hands were wide; his nails were chipped and ingrained with black, and his finger-

94

tips were almost flat, as though they'd been squashed under a heavy weight.

On one cheek, the word GOLD was tattooed in fine black letters into his pockmarked skin.

Granite stepped forward and their eyes locked: Copper's dark brown ones and his coal black ones. For a moment they battled silently, each assessing the other, each preparing to fight.

Copper didn't let her gaze drop, although her insides were weak and wobbly.

Then Granite lumbered toward her on bent, knobbly legs, like an old crippled toad, licking his thin wide mouth as if she were a juicy fly he was coming to eat.

"It's been a long time since I've seen you, little stick, and how you've changed. Copper Beech," he croaked. "Now, there's an interesting name. A freaky name. A combination— metal and wood."

"I'm not a freak. Copper Beech is a tree," said Copper, sticking out her chin proudly. "And if I am both wood and metal, well, other things are—a knife, a cart, lots of things."

"Huh!"

"I'm not afraid, you know," she said, and it was almost true.

"Not afraid? Ha! You will be," growled Granite, scrunching his hands together and cracking their joints. "Everyone is afraid of me. I am Lord of the Rock and molten lead runs through my veins! Mercury courses through my arteries, and my heart is hewn from steel!"

Copper stepped back involuntarily.

"Your father was so afraid that he ran away and never came back. Your mother was so afraid, she . . ."

Copper felt a wave of icy goose pimples spreading up and down her spine.

"What? What about my mother?"

Granite grinned nastily. "You'd like to know about your mother, wouldn't you? Wouldn't you?"

Copper stared down at the floor. If Granite realized how badly she wanted to know, it would be like showing him a raw wound and he could hurt her all the more.

"You said you weren't afraid. You can't even look me in the eye!" croaked Granite.

"I can. I will . . ." Copper hesitated. Her hands were scrabbling in her pocket, searching. Her fingers were itching to dance and fly. She felt loose and weak, and if she didn't do something in a few seconds, all would be lost. "I just have to . . . Excuse me."

At last she found her crochet hook and blue wool and quickly cast on some stitches. In, out, in, out. The needle danced expertly.

Granite gazed at her. His face was unmoving, his eyes unblinking.

"Triple loop, hook in and out, slip one over and in, out . . . ," muttered Copper. "That's better. Just a few stitches. I'm not afraid. If I don't look at you, it's because I prefer not to look at you. You aren't very nice to look at and you're trying to threaten me." She glanced up at Granite, then continued crocheting.

Granite stared, then, pushing aside a heap of pearls and other precious stones, settled himself on the edge of a table, watching her.

This time Copper stared back.

"Is your knitting as good as your crocheting?" he asked gruffly.

"Of course."

"Is it indeed? Do you know why I brought you here, Copper Beech?"

"I haven't a clue," she said calmly. In, out, in, out, twist, loop, over and through, her needle went as if on a journey of its own.

"You've got something I want, Copper. Look! You can see how I like my gold, see how I've filled the room with lovely things, delicious ornaments and brooches and brilliant bangles."

Copper felt the blood beginning to rise in her cheeks: he was going to ask about the charm bracelet.

"I'm a reasonable man. I don't want to hurt you. I'll swap you." He leaned lower toward her, dropping his voice. "Take what you want from here, I've got mountains of the stuff. Take anything. All I want in exchange is that little charm bracelet you've got. It's not worth a jot compared with all this. Come on, give it to me!"

He held out one of his broad, black-stained hands.

"Give it to me!"

Copper didn't move. Suddenly his steely fingers locked around her arm like a vise, and he yanked her toward him until his face, tilted down at hers, was just inches away. She couldn't help but see how his skin was marked with millions of tiny holes and lumps, like blackened orange peel. How his hair was greasy and how his breath smelled of stagnant water.

"I'm talking to you, Copper Beech!"

"No," said Copper. "I've been to the theater. I've seen *Aladdin* hundreds of times, and that's just what his wicked uncle Abanazer says. That bracelet must be worth loads and loads if you want it so badly. And anyway, I haven't got it. I don't know what you're talking about."

"Liar!" he gasped. "Liar. Of course you've got it—somewhere. What did you come to the Marble Mountains for if you haven't got it?" Keeping hold of her arm, he hauled her roughly out of the room.

Locking the metal door behind them, he half dragged her down the stone corridor to another miserable, gray room where two unsmiling women were waiting for them. They wore gray clothes and hats, beneath which their faces were gray and tired.

"Search her!" he said.

The women came slowly toward Copper and took hold of her. With their backs turned to Granite, they whispered to her, "Sorry, dear."

Then they began looking through all her clothes, in her boots and socks, under her sweaters and in all her pockets.

"There's knitting wool," they said. "And a crochet needle."

Granite shook his head irritably. "I know. I know. What else?"

"A gold charm," cried one woman, finding it in Copper's trouser pocket.

Granite smiled and held out his hand, open palmed. "That's more like it," he said. "I knew . . ." But his face changed when he saw that it was the tiny fir tree charm.

"Where did you get it?"

"I found it."

"Did you? I sent that charm to your mother. Yes, it was a little present for her. I thought it had gone long ago. Do you like it? The mighty ax cuts down the weak tree. It signifies the destruction of the Wood family by the Stone family. Hard against soft. What wonderful stone buildings we Rockers have built: the pyramids, the temples, Stonehenge, even. But the Woods . . . nothing. I hope Amber liked it."

"She didn't. I found it on top of the curtains. I bet she was throwing it out the window and it got caught up there," said Copper in a flash of inspiration. "It's ugly."

"There must be more," said Granite to the women. "Go on, keep searching!"

"Yes, Granite," the women muttered.

Copper stood very still. She had been holding Ralick in her arms, and now he hung, dangling in her hand.

Oh, please, not Ralick, she begged silently. Please, please, if I don't look at him or think about him at all, perhaps they won't touch him.

"Nothing." Both women stepped back.

Granite smiled nastily at Copper. "Very well, now try that revolting, bald old teddy," he said. "She's far too old for a toy like that anyway. Pull it to pieces!"

17. Granite's Secret

"Don't! Not Ralick! Please!"

Copper held him against her chest where it seemed his heart beat as rapidly as hers. "He's all I've got."

"Really? You wouldn't be hiding something in him, would you?"

"No, no! I don't know anything about a bracelet."

She held on to him tightly, silently telling him it would be all right. She wouldn't let them hurt him, but there was nothing she could do. The women pried her fingers from him and took him away.

It was like removing a part of her. Never had she felt so bad or been so scared.

She didn't want them to find the bracelet, but she didn't want them to harm Ralick. Which was worse? Which mattered most?

Copper held her breath.

The women carefully took off Ralick's hat. Copper's heart seemed to take one long last beat, then held on, waiting.

Would they feel the charm bracelet inside the knitted cuff? Would they?

They took off the hat, looked inside it, then tossed it to the floor.

Copper's heart began beating again and she breathed once more.

"Shall we open it up?" asked one woman.

"There's nothing there," said Copper. "Please. I promise. He's empty."

They were holding Ralick tightly, stretching him, and a dreadful popping sound meant the stitches in Ralick's seam were breaking. It was like a jolt of electricity through Copper. "Please!" she cried.

"Yes, yes," said Granite, never taking his fathomless black eyes off Copper, "that's right. I'm sure it's in there."

"He's empty. I promise," said Copper. "Please don't."

Ignoring her, one of the women took a large, sharp knife and, sticking it straight into his tummy, sliced open the seam along Ralick's front and pulled out his stuffing.

"Ralick!"

It was dreadful! Terrible to see him pulled apart like that, as if he were just a toy. Copper clutched at her own stomach in sympathy. Poor Ralick.

They squashed him and prodded him and shook him upside down.

"Nothing," one woman said.

"Give him to me!" snapped Granite. "It must be in there. Useless . . . Go on, go!"

The women shuffled out.

Granite squeezed Ralick's arms and legs, feeling for the slightest lump or hardness. He searched in every corner of the toy and ripped out more of his filling. Finally, he flung Ralick back at Copper. "Nothing!" he said grimly. "Nothing. Here, have your teddy back and stop looking at me like that; it's only a stuffed toy!"

Copper gathered Ralick into her arms. Only a stuffed toy? What did he know? How could he ever appreciate the hours that Ralick and Copper had spent together? The secrets they'd told each other?

"I told you I didn't have the bracelet," said Copper calmly, although inside she was trembling as if *her* stuffing had been pulled out. She picked up Ralick's pale fluff from the floor and pushed it gently back into his middle. She retrieved his hat and tied it back on neatly.

"I'll mend you," she whispered. "Dear Ralick. You are brave."

"Never knew I had it in me," wheezed Ralick. "If you see what I mean."

"This isn't a game, Stick, this is for real," snapped Granite. "You've got that bracelet and I need it. I'm going to get it."

He turned and began lumbering up and down the room, muttering to himself. When he turned back, he was smirking.

"About *Amber,* did they explain?"

Copper shook her head.

"You know the Wood and the Stone families were once . . . friends?"

Copper nodded.

"That was until your family got greedy. Your great-grandfather Ash cheated us. Surprised? You think your family is so wonderful, don't you? But it's true. Ash stole our gold, which was payment for wooden goods we never got. He disappeared with it. He ran away. That's the sort of person he was. Is it any wonder that Cedar was such a coward? You're all the same. *You run away,* you hide. Cowards!"

"I'm not!" cried Copper. "And I don't believe you anyway. Why should I believe anything you say?"

"Because it's the truth. Show me it's not true and I might forgive. Your family stole from us and wouldn't admit it. So we stopped trading. You had our metal goods and they last for years, but we had to do without wooden things. We had to cut down trees ourselves and it doesn't come easy . . . and then we couldn't do anything with them. It's not in our blood to carve wood. Now we have nothing."

"I . . . ," began Copper.

"Wait. There's more. I've got plenty against your family, Stick, plenty. I had an older sister, Pearl. She married a Wood. I begged her not to, but she did it anyway and I refused to see her ever again. Then Amber did the same. Amber, down there in Spindle House! With those people who had cheated us! Traitor! She had food and warmth and everything she wanted, and we had nothing. I fought Cedar. Your mother came with me. She *volunteered* to come back to the Rock with me. She didn't really care about him. She brought you to be with me and then . . ."

"Then *what?*" Copper couldn't help asking. She saw her mistake immediately when Granite leaned toward her, smiling nastily.

"You really are interested in knowing about your dear mother, aren't you?" He chuckled. "Shall I show you? Amber got the better of me. She always did. Come with me, come on, I do *so* want to show you!"

He pulled her along winding corridors until they reached some narrow steps that led downward. Grabbing a lighted lantern from the wall, he hustled her along with him and descended into the darkness.

"Are you scared, little wooden thing? You should be excited. You're going to find out about your mother at last!"

The rough rock walls glistened with water seeping through the cracks. The rock floor was wet and slippery. The farther down they went, the colder it became. Icicles hung from the roof and ice glistened on the walls. Copper's breath blossomed in a cloud around her face. The cold air caught in her throat and froze in her nose.

"Yes, it's cold, isn't it? They say the mountains are getting colder. They say that trees will never grow on these hills again. Your fault. You Woods have done it!"

Copper didn't reply. She was so cold her brain seemed to have stopped working. She was no longer afraid. She followed Granite blindly. He was going to lead her to her mother. That was the only important thing. The only thing she cared about.

At the bottom of the stairs, the air was moist. The sound of water lapping against rocks filled the air.

The light was very poor, but as Copper took a few tentative steps forward, she sensed a vast emptiness in front of her as the ceiling soared upward out of sight.

"The lake freezes up some years," said Granite, as if talking to himself. "Like the year that you came. Very cold. Come on, this way."

Granite led her along the side of the lake, then turned off down a wide tunnel to where a shallow cave was set into the rock wall.

At the back of the cave, a sheet of ice hung from the ceiling to the floor in frozen pleats and folds like a solid green and blue curtain. Granite was pulling her toward the ice, but Copper hung back, afraid. There was something in the ice, something terrible.

"Look!" he hissed.

Trembling, Copper drew nearer. "I can't . . ."

She looked back at Granite; his mouth was a twisted smile. If a forked tongue had slithered out it wouldn't have surprised her.

"Please . . . ," she begged in a whisper.

"There! Look deep into the ice," he said. "See the blue ice pillar deep inside? The ice inside the ice and inside that . . . Can't you see her? Can't you see her there, Copper? That's your mother!"

18. Amber

Copper swallowed. Her mouth was dry. She laid a hand over her heart, hoping to calm it. "My mother?" she gasped. "Dead?"

Copper took a tentative step nearer. Then another. Peering all the time into the beautiful iridescent ice, trying to look through it and into it and yet afraid of what she might see.

"Is that really my mother?"

The woman's features were hard to make out. Large brown eyes, a strong chin and a wide, pale face. Her right arm was held out; her eyes stared away past Copper.

"So sad," said Copper. "And wistful. She's reaching out for something."

Her long, wild hair floated in a still cloud round her face, like seaweed tossed and curling in a frozen current. Her ankle-length dress ballooned as if full of air.

Copper saw a glint of greenish gold on the woman's wrist and drew in her breath sharply. "I think it really is her."

Granite leaped forward. He had been watching her carefully. "Ah ha! You saw her bracelet, didn't you? I gave her that bracelet," he croaked. "I made it. I designed and fashioned every single charm, and I made her wear it. It won't ever come off. You could say it's the most expensive handcuff in the world."

"But you didn't make mine!"

"Ha! So you *do* have the charm bracelet!" snapped Granite. "I knew it. I knew she must have given it to you."

"Aunt Ruby gave it to me."

"But Amber made it."

"Amber made it?" repeated Copper breathlessly. "My mother made it for me?" The words brought a warmth flooding through her that made her skin tingle all over. She broke into a smile. "I'm so *happy* it was her."

"She was a genius with gold," said Granite crossly. "Such a talent. Such finesse."

"What did you do to her?"

"Nothing. It's suspended animation," growled Granite. "Nothing to do with me. She did it herself, some trickery to keep herself from me. But she's a Stone and she belongs here and here she'll stay. Free from me," said Granite. "Free from you, from Cedar, everyone. She didn't want any of you."

"That's dreadful," said Copper, looking anxiously from her mother to Granite and back again. "She loved Cedar. I'm sure she loved me. She looks so very sad. . . . I think she was *too* sad to go on. You made her sad, and she's locked herself away from the sadness, and it's all your fault."

Granite laughed nastily. "Maybe, maybe. I think she was a wicked girl and did this to punish me. She wouldn't do what I wanted, but now at last you're here."

"Why can't you get her out? Why can't we melt the ice and break it down and get her out?"

Granite took hold of Copper's wrist and squeezed it tightly.

"You stupid girl," he hissed, his face close to hers. "I cannot get her out of that ice prison because she put herself in there. The only way she will be released is by you—you and the gold charm bracelet." He let go of her suddenly, his voice softening into a wheedling whisper. "Only you can free your mother, Copper. This is what you need to do. You *need* to save your mother, so don't tell me you don't have the gold bracelet. You must have it!" He paused and wiped his face, trying to calm himself. "When she's free it will be the end of the quarrel. All over and done with. We can be friends. Your mother would want that."

"Is that true?"

But Granite had turned away and was lumbering back down the tunnel.

"Come on, Stick. Follow me. There's plenty of time to think about it."

Then Copper had a sudden flash of inspiration.

Seeing Granite's retreating back, she quickly reached for her ball of wool and slipped the looped end of it over an icicle. It was done in an instant and Granite didn't see a thing. Then, as she followed him out, the wool in her pocket slowly unraveled, leaving a blue line. Now I can come back and find her all by myself, she thought. I'll set you free, Amber. I can do it.

"Go back to your room," Granite said, "and think about what I've told you. I'll leave you a few days. I should imagine that without food and drink you will soon come round to seeing things my way."

The door slammed behind Copper and she was alone in her cell again.

"Ralick." Copper gathered him into her arms. "My mother is here!" Quickly she told him what she'd seen and what Granite had told her. "I feel all unraveled," she added. "And yet coming together too."

"*You* feel unraveled," said Ralick indignantly. "You don't know the meaning of the word. I'm coming apart at the seams. Loose. Frayed at the edges . . ."

"Oh, Ralick, I'm sorry. Look, I'll wrap my hankie round you," said Copper. She bound her large hankie round his middle and tied it tightly. "That'll hold things in a bit."

"Thanks," said Ralick. "It's all mighty suspicious," he went on. "Why does Granite want Amber set free? I mean, why not leave her in the ice? He's got her, your father doesn't."

"It could be just that he loves her . . ."

"Nah," said Ralick.

"So what shall we do?"

"Escape," said Ralick. "That's what we shall do."

110

"Ralick, that's a very good idea," said Copper, looking round the tiny room. "But how? The door's locked. . . ."

"Try your crochet hook."

"Another brilliant idea, Ralick," she said, jumping off the bed. She slipped the long hooked needle into the lock. "This is the sort of thing that people do in films," Copper whispered, "but I never thought I'd be doing it. How does it work?"

Suddenly, *click,* the hook caught and turned and the lock was undone.

"Like that!" said Ralick.

"Amazing. Off we go." Copper snuggled Ralick down the front of her coat, put her crochet hook back in her pocket and crept out.

The corridor was empty. Above her the hazy green vapor shimmered brightly. The walls glistened moist and cold. A bitter draft nipped at her legs.

"This way," she whispered. "Down the corridor and then we should find my wool on the stairs."

"You hope," growled Ralick.

"That's right, Ralick, I hope. Let's try to be positive."

As Copper slipped along the passageway, an eruption of loud, angry voices and hammering noises stopped her. She shrank back against the wall and held her breath, listening. From outside the Rock she could hear yells and shouting— that was surely her father's voice! Yes, and Questrid too!

They must be at the front door! The hammering echoed

and reverberated through the cavernous building. Doors slammed, and inside the Rock there was the scurrying of many feet along the stone corridors and more shouting.

"My father and Questrid, they've come to rescue us," breathed Copper, looking back to where the commotion was coming from.

"Let's go and be rescued, then," said Ralick.

"No. I can't. I have to help my mother."

"You can't be serious."

"I am. Oh, Ralick, it's great that Cedar came to find me, I'm proud of him, I *love* him for it, but they'll never get in the Rock. How can they? And this may be my only chance to get Amber out."

"But Copper . . ."

"No, I've made up my mind. I'm going to Amber."

Copper scampered off along the corridor. She took a lantern down from its bracket on the wall and, reaching the stairs, descended quickly into the darkness.

At the bottom, near the path leading to the lake, Copper picked up the end of the wool she'd left. She sighed with relief. Anyone might have found it. But they hadn't. She was safe.

She ran quickly, reeling in the wool and balling it up as she went. Her heart was racing now, like horses' hooves galloping in her chest, and she felt hot and clumsy inside her thick coat.

I'm coming, she thought. I've got the charms. There's nothing to stop me. I'll save you now, Mother, and then we'll go to Cedar and be together like a real family and I'll have done it all. My mother . . . oh!

She stopped suddenly. "Did you hear something, Ralick?"

"Nothing except your blooming heart going like a piston in my earhole."

Copper took a few more steps: the light was very dim and the air misty with moisture from the lake.

She stopped again, trembling: there was a noise. Someone was there.

She darted forward, pulling at the wool, but the sound of hurrying footsteps was gaining on her, coming nearer, nearer. She froze, waiting for the heavy hand on her shoulder, the cold voice of Granite . . . then . . .

"Copper!"

She spun round in amazement.

"Questrid! Questrid, is it you?" she marveled. "It *is* you! How did you find me?" She threw her arms round him, knocking his hat to the floor. "It's so good to see you, you've no idea! How did you find me?"

Questrid grinned, and at that moment Copper thought it was the nicest, jolliest smile in the whole world.

"We were out searching for Silver," Questrid explained in a loud whisper. "Didn't even know you'd gone, when we heard the alarm. We thought it might be a fire, or rock rolling, but it wasn't, and then we saw your footsteps in the snow and the sled marks, so we knew you'd been captured. We all came up to the Rock—even your father—and started shouting and trying to break open the door. It looks shoddy, but it sure is strong! Then the Rockers started yelling and chucking stones out the windows and we had to go back. . . . Well, the others did. I dodged round the stones and sneaked in through a broken window. This place is a real dump."

"But how did you find me here?"

"Oh, I tracked you. I hunted you down."

"Am I really so smelly?"

"You certainly are. You can follow a strand of wool, Copper, and I can follow a smell. And I found something really interesting. Come and see."

"Oh, not now, Questrid, we've no time, they might be following us. They might come and get us any moment."

"It'll only take a sec. Come on. You must see, it's so weird." And he pulled her round a corner to where a small metal door was set into the rock. From all around it, the brilliant green light shone brightly, as if it were trying to push its way out from the inside.

"What is it?"

"Come and see," Questrid insisted.

The key was in the lock and he quickly opened the door.

Green light poured out like liquid, bathing them in color and making them blink.

"This is where it comes from," he said. "There's a sort of hole or well in the floor, see? I can't imagine what it is. The green comes out and up all those cracks and pipes in the ceiling and then all over the Rock, I guess. Isn't it weird?"

"Yes. Fantastic! But now, come with *me*, Questrid. I've got something to show you, and if we don't hurry, Granite will be after us."

She pulled him away and, following the wool trail again, made toward the underground lake.

They had left the door of the green light room open, letting a wave of colored air waft along behind them. Everything shimmered greenly, like sunshine coming through a thick canopy of leaves.

At last they reached the cave. "Here, this way, she's in here," cried Copper. "Questrid . . . It's my mother."

Questrid gazed at the ice in amazement. He took a few steps back, then a few forward, resting his nose right against the ice to stare inside.

"Blimey!"

"Granite told me I was the only one who can set her free," said Copper, undoing her coat and pulling Ralick out. She began ripping open the stitches around Ralick's hat. "She's alive in there, Questrid, and I'm going to set her free, with this." She held out the bracelet. "There!"

It was like a handful of fireworks, fizzing and sparkling, glittering and glowing as if charged with electricity.

"Wow!" said Questrid.

"Poor Ralick, he said it had—I mean," Copper added, realizing her blunder, "Ralick was hiding it. I didn't notice it was so, so brilliant!"

"It's like it's on fire!" cried Questrid. "It's beauti—"

Suddenly a horrible, grating laugh resounded across the cave, hammering their ears and pounding into their heads.

"Ah ha ha! Ha ha haaa!"

It was Granite. He rose up slowly from behind a jutting rock like a genie, with an evil smile on his lips.

"Thank you, *Stick,* thank you very much. That's the bracelet I want. How extremely kind and thoughtful of you to bring it into the Rock for me."

19. ACROSS THE LAKE

GRANITE WADDLED OUT from behind the rock, but Copper quickly darted out of his way. She pushed the bracelet deep into her pocket, stuffed Ralick back down her coat and sped back toward the lake.

Granite swung round, grabbing at her, but didn't see the wool still stretched across the doorway: he tripped over it and fell, crashing to the floor with a heavy thud.

"RUN!" cried Questrid.

They ran. They ran, half skating on the icy floor, leaping over rocks and dodging the spiked icicles that hung from the ceiling. Back along the path they went until, panting, they came to the lake.

Green light had flooded through the open door and lit up the whole massive cavern. Even the lake water was emerald. Each tiny moving point in the water glinted turquoise and green and was reflected eerily in shimmering dots over the walls and ceiling.

"Look, there's a boat," said Questrid, pointing to a small

wooden rowboat tied up between the rocks. "Quick!" He wrenched the boat free from the chunks of ice that had gathered at the shore and pulled it near so Copper could jump in.

Copper yelped as she made contact with the wood. It was such a shock, like jumping into a living thing: as her fingers touched its sides, the boat gave a minute throb and shudder in response.

"For Wood people," she whispered.

Questrid leaped in behind Copper, unhooked the rope and pushed off from the rocks with an oar. The boat wavered off across the water.

A few seconds later, Granite appeared at the lakeside. He was bent over and gasping for breath.

"You'll never escape!" Granite called to them wheezily. But he didn't try to stop them. He crouched beside the water, legs apart, watching.

Minutes later, the cave filled with the thundering noise of feet, and twenty or thirty Rockers burst in. They climbed the craggy walls to stand on high ledges and ridges circling the lake. Then they too watched silently as Questrid and Copper rowed across the water.

"Oh, heck, look at that lot," whispered Questrid, squinting round over his shoulder.

"What shall we do?" gasped Copper.

"Get me out of here," whispered Ralick from inside her coat.

"Pray there are no more boats," said Questrid, "and that there's a way out of this place."

Peering into the gloom ahead, Questrid rowed the little boat through the lumps of bobbing ice, as far away from the shore as possible.

"It's like riding a horse," said Questrid in awe. "I can feel the boat trying to understand me and guess which way I want to go, but I don't know myself."

"There's something there," said Copper, pointing. "Look, a big black hole. A tunnel, I think. Can we get through?"

"We can try."

Questrid turned the boat and headed toward the tunnel entrance. "Yeah, plenty of room," he called out.

"What's that?" Copper nodded toward a tall, thin column that rose out of the water.

"Just a sort of tall stone," said Questrid.

"Odd place for a tall stone," said Copper, "right in front of the tunnel like that. Funny shape too, with that big stone on the top, like a hat." She looked up at the silent men, standing around the cavern walls. "Why aren't they doing anything? I hate this quiet. Why are they just watching us? What d'you think they're planning?"

"I've got a bad feeling in my seams," hissed Ralick.

Copper gave him a reassuring squeeze.

Questrid shrugged. "Nothing, I don't think. They're probably just mad that we're getting away—if it is a way out," he added. "We're nearly there now."

They were just five meters from the tunnel when a mighty roar went up and suddenly the cave was filled with sound and activity.

"NOW!" roared Granite, and as if by magic, a vast net swung down in front of the tunnel entrance, blocking off their escape.

Copper shrieked.

Ralick shrieked very quietly.

"No!" cried Questrid. The oars fell from his grasp and the little boat dipped and spun in a crazy circle, like a beetle flipped on its back. Quickly Questrid caught the oars again and began rowing back toward the center of the lake.

"What are we going to do?"

Copper looked over to Granite. He hadn't moved. He waved at them, grinning.

"Thank you for falling so neatly into my trap," he called. "I knew you had the bracelet somewhere. I knew you'd go to Amber and try to set her free. Greedy, greedy little Stick. Now, come over here and bring it to me."

"Ignore him," said Questrid.

Copper took the bracelet out of her pocket. It was fizzing and sparkling.

"It's really crackling," she said. "It seems to draw energy from being here. It was never like this before."

"As if it's turned on," agreed Questrid. "This is how it was when it was near your mother, wasn't it? Do you think we can use it somehow? I mean, if it's magical enough to get

Amber out of the ice, like Granite says, then it must be magical enough to get us out of this. But how?"

"COPPER!" Granite's rough voice interrupted them. "You're wasting time! Come here!"

Copper ignored him. She let the bracelet dribble through her fingers, marveling at the way it trickled like gold water and the way tiny dots of gold flew off like sparks from a fire. "It's so beautiful."

"Yes, but make it do something," urged Questrid.

"What?" Copper scanned the charms hopefully. "There are two babies, a dog, a bird, a heart, a hammer . . ."

"HAMMER?"

"Yes, a teeny-weeny hammer, Questrid, it can't possibly do any good."

"Of course it will!"

Copper grinned. "Of course it will. Amber made it for a purpose. Now, what do people hit with hammers?"

"A nail?" came Ralick's whispered suggestion.

"Yes, but we haven't . . ."

"Are you talking to me, Copper?" said Questrid.

"No. Yes! That's it! Row back to that funny, tall stone thing, Questrid. It's not a funny stone at all. It's a nail!"

"What? D'you really think so?"

"Yes. A nail for hammering."

Ignoring the jeers and shouts from the Rockers, they rowed back to the giant nail-like stone.

Questrid tried to steady the boat as Copper got to her feet.

Holding the tiny hammer in her fingers, she leaned toward the column. The boat bobbed up and down.

"Shall I?"

"STOP!" roared Granite. "Don't do that! You don't know what it might do! Stop. STOP!"

Copper smiled grimly. "Good, he's worried. I think this was a good idea."

Carefully, she struck the top of the rock with the tiny hammer.

Immediately a clear sound like the chime of an expensive clock rang out around the cave and the nail seemed to sink ever so slightly into the water.

"Do it again," said Questrid.

"NO!" yelled Granite.

"Yes," urged Questrid.

Copper hit the rock again.

This time there was a dull, distant noise like thunder followed by a roaring like a train rushing toward them. The water shivered and the rocks shuddered. The nail sank farther.

"Yes, yes, yes!" cried Questrid. "Something's happening. Do it again, do it again!"

"But . . . what about my mother?"

Copper looked back at Granite and could feel his anger reaching to her across the water. His eyes were black holes in his pale face.

"Later," said Questrid. "I promise we'll get Amber later."

Copper hit the rock a third time.

A roar, as if a jumbo jet were picking up speed to take off inside a hollow box, thundered and crashed and blasted the air around them. The nail slithered and sank, disappearing into the water with a slow, deep gurgle.

Then the cave was full of flying rocks and stones and grit and dust. The Rockers shouted and yelled, swarming over the rock ledges like angry ants.

A great swell rose under them, and Copper clung to the sides of the boat as it was lifted on a great wave like the back of a whale.

"That was some hammer!" cried Questrid as the boat soared toward the roof. Then suddenly they were plunging downward again, icy water sprayed over them, and Questrid had to grab for the oars before they were tossed overboard.

"Look!" he cried. "The men are on the net. It's sagging. It's going to break!"

Trying to escape the falling rocks, the men clambered over the net, clinging to it like monkeys. But there were too many of them, and bit by bit, the net was beginning to slip into the lake.

"If it falls, we'll be able to . . . There! It's down!" she cried as the net finally fell. The Rockers toppled into the water with splashes and shouts and began swimming toward the shore.

Questrid strained against the oars, crashing through the choppy waves as the water rose and fell and swirled beneath them. He pointed the boat toward the mouth of the now unblocked tunnel.

"Uh-oh," said Questrid quietly, "more trouble. Look behind you."

Copper twisted round quickly.

Something was speeding up behind them—a huddle of boats or rocks . . . no, it was great slabs of ice, globs of sharp blue ice, spinning and twisting through the wild water.

"Look out!"

"I don't think I'm going to like this," moaned Ralick.

The ice splinters skimmed up behind them and hit the boat with a mighty smash, jolting them so fiercely that Copper would have tipped out if the wooden boat hadn't been gripping her fingers so firmly.

The mouth of the tunnel loomed up, and Questrid yanked in the oars just before they sped inside.

The tunnel was narrow, and the water moved quickly, roaring, screaming. They went faster and faster.

"Hang on!" cried Questrid. "Hang on!"

The boat was caught in a tidal wave, it was lifted and carried along, grazing the rock walls, tipping and dipping, shooting forward, then round in a dizzying whirl. Behind them, like an angry animal, came the mass of creaking, groaning ice.

Copper was numb with cold and fright. We're going to die, she thought. This is it. The end, and I've hardly begun . . .

"It's all right," whispered Ralick. "It's only like the rides at the fair."

In her mind's eye Copper saw Spindle House. She smelled the sandalwood in the sitting room, the apple wood in her bedroom; she saw her father's face, the mother's face she would never know . . .

"But I must know her!" she shouted and immediately the panic melted away and she knew, she absolutely knew that she couldn't give up, because she *was* going to see her mother again and she *was* going to know her.

20. HOME AGAIN

THE WATER THUNDERED around them, pounding, swishing and tossing them like toys in a tub, but it no longer scared Copper: she was going to win.

She smiled at the biting cold of the water as it splashed her skin. She grinned at the vicious ice behind them that threatened to crush them at any moment.

"Are you all right?" cried Questrid, alarmed by Copper's frozen smile. He had stashed the oars at the bottom of the boat and, like Copper, was gripping the sides and staring ahead into the darkness. He was damp and shivering.

"Yes!" she shouted back. "Don't worry. It'll be all right."

She wanted to shout, I've got a mother and a father, just like I always knew I had. I've found them at last. But she only smiled.

"Look, there's light up ahead. Daylight," cried Questrid.

"I see it," said Copper. "I knew it would be all right. I just knew it."

The circle of light grew brighter and larger as they sped toward it. Then, suddenly, they were at the end of the tunnel and the wave gushed out, like water from a burst pipe. Questrid and Copper popped out into the fresh air, screaming and shouting.

There was nothing in front of them now except the snow-covered hill stretching out below.

Copper tensed, ready for the boat to crash onto the ground, but it didn't. The wave of water had thrown them down onto the hillside, and as the water met the freezing air it turned to ice beneath them, and now the boat was speeding down the hillside, sailing on a frozen ice river.

"Yahoo!" Questrid cried, pulling himself onto his knees in the prow. "Yahoo!"

The boat tipped and tilted as it slithered down the blue and silver mountainside, smooth as glass, toward Spindle House far below.

The boat was going home.

"Wheeeee!" cheered Ralick, peeping through the front of Copper's coat.

Behind them, the great shards and blocks of ice pushed and bounced and tumbled along as if trying to catch up. Looking back, Copper half expected to see Granite and his men somersaulting along among the ice, but there was no sign of them, they were safe inside the Rock.

At last the boat slid slowly into the courtyard where everyone was waiting for them.

"Copper! Questrid! We saw the ice. We saw it all falling and we didn't know . . . ," cried Oriole, rushing to them and hugging them.

"Oh, thank goodness you're back."

"What's been going on?"

"Copper? Questrid, are you all right?"

They pulled them out of the boat and kissed them and hugged them.

It was a hard moment for Copper. The one and only time she'd seen her father, she had run away from him, and now she didn't know what to do. She avoided meeting his gaze, and when Cedar touched her, she was as solid as a tree trunk in his arms. Pretending she'd dropped her crochet needle in the boat, she went back to it, to have a moment alone.

"What's the matter?" hissed Ralick.

"Nothing. Just avoiding someone, that's all."

In case she was being watched, she pretended to search the boat. Of course there was nothing there, but she saw something she hadn't noticed before: the boat's name. Carved in intricate letters on the little boat's prow was the name LINDEN.

Copper was astonished. Was *this* the Linden she had to be kind to? Was it possible to be kind to a boat? But it was a Linden who had been kind to them and saved them from Granite. I'm sure Aunt Ruby said a person called Linden, she thought. What's the connection? Silver. Linden. Amber and Cedar . . . She looked up at her father, who was watching her, and then away. What could she say to him? Would they ever be able to say anything to each other?

Quickly she followed the others into the kitchen, which smelled wonderful—of new bread and wood smoke. The birds twittered noisily. When Questrid and Copper had put on dry clothes, they sat by the fire and sipped hot chocolate. Copper propped Ralick up against the warm stove to dry, and Questrid described his part of the adventure.

"Well done, Questrid," said Cedar, when he'd finished. "It was very brave of you to go into the Rock. I wish I could have fit through that broken window."

"You should have seen your father, Copper," Oriole said. "He made such a fuss and banged and yelled. But we couldn't get in. The Rock's as impenetrable as a fort."

"We were going to send the birds in to drop smoke bombs," said Robin. "We contemplated setting fire to the wooden bits but we worried about hurting you."

"We didn't want to endanger you," said Cedar. "We were going to go back with reinforcements."

"Thank you for trying," said Copper quietly, staring at her feet. "Oriole, I do so want Aunt Ruby to come. I need her. Could Robin send a message with one of his birds, do you think?"

Oriole nodded. "Of course. Now, can you tell us what happened to you?"

Copper told them, starting at the beginning when she had been enticed out of the garden by Silver.

"Silver!" cried Oriole. "But she would *never . . .*"

"I know," agreed Copper. "She didn't look happy at all. . . . I think she'd had her puppies and I think the Rockers must have kept them from her. It's the only thing I can think of."

Then Copper repeated what Granite had told her about Great-Grandfather Ash stealing their gold. Uncle Greenwood looked embarrassed.

"It could be true," admitted Cedar, meeting Copper's gaze. "But I can't believe it myself. I think he was a good man, but . . . the truth is, he did disappear and so did all the gold, but he might have had an accident. People do get lost up there, fall down ravines or get caught in snowfalls."

"Did anyone look for him?"

Greenwood nodded. "I remember our father telling us about the searches that went on, but I was only a small boy then. He never believed the Rockers had given Ash the gold in the first place. There was bad feeling on both sides, you see? And it grew and grew. No one is entirely bad or entirely good, but events can push you one way or the other."

"Granite seems to blame the Wood family for every misfortune he's had," said Copper.

Cedar nodded. "He was beside himself with anger when I married Amber. It wasn't the first time a Wood had gone off with a Rock. His own sister did it, so the hatred was already there."

"But . . ." Copper was confused. "Why was it worse for Granite when Amber married you?"

Cedar opened his mouth, but didn't say anything.

"Was he in love with her?" asked Copper.

"Perhaps. Maybe he thought he was. I can't believe he could ever love anything."

"Can't you? Don't you believe anything he says? Why else would he want her free of the ice unless he loved her? If he loved her, he can't be all bad, can he? If he *loves* her, I mean."

Cedar looked uncomfortable. "If," he repeated quietly.

An awkward hush fell until Oriole said, "I can't help thinking about our poor Silver, trapped up there in the Rock with her puppies just born and everything. She's such a good dog . . ."

"*Wolf,* you know she's a wolf!" said Copper crossly. "You can stop pretending now."

Now Oriole looked uncomfortable.

"I'm sorry we didn't tell you," said Robin. "I imagine it feels like we tricked you, but we didn't want to scare you. I am sorry."

"Silver belonged to Amber," said Cedar. "Amber found her starving in a cave and brought her home and nursed her. Silver would never do anything to hurt Amber. She'd rather die."

"So the Rockers have her and her puppies," said Questrid.

"And Silver will do anything the Rockers want."

"Poor Silver, those poor babies," said Oriole. "And they must still be up there in that dreadful, cold stone place."

It was a strange day. Copper felt restless and unhappy.

"Everyone knows everything and I know nothing," she told Oriole. "All these secrets that they share. It's not fair."

"I suppose Robin and I did know about your father," admitted Oriole. "But we also didn't. We were part of the secret and yet we were not. Nobody told us. When we came to live here, there was only Greenwood. I sent food upstairs, but I never asked why."

"It was safer for Cedar that way, I suppose," said Copper.

"Yes. But I wish we'd told you. Or that they had told you," said Oriole. "Still, you've started to change things. You've shaken us all up, stopped us from behaving so stupidly. You should be proud of yourself."

But Copper wasn't proud of herself, and she was sure that her father wasn't either. Her running away had not been brave.

She sat in the kitchen and knitted three socks for Ralick— none of which fit—a bit of a tea cozy and three fingers of a glove, then pulled everything out.

"I wish I knew what I wanted to knit," she moaned. "I need a pattern, that's what I need, but I don't know what of. . . . Oh, I can't stop thinking about Amber still up there in the ice. She must be so cold! We shouldn't have left her. Or Silver."

"Imagine being so miserable that your only way out is to lock yourself up in the cold, cold ice." Oriole shivered. "Poor Amber. A terrible choice. But we'll get her out somehow."

"You know what else," Copper went on. "It was so odd, just being there, knowing I half belonged there, since I am half a Stone person and half a Wood person. I mean, Granite seemed to hate me for being a mixture, but actually I think it's the best."

"So do I," agreed Questrid.

"What did happen when I was four? Only Aunt Ruby can tell me. Dear Aunt Ruby, she's so good at sorting things out. I do hope she comes soon."

"I don't suppose I'm of any use," said her father suddenly.

Copper jumped up in surprise. Cedar had slipped into the kitchen very quietly.

"Oh, it's you."

"Yes, just me. Copper, will you come into the sitting room and talk to me? I need to talk to you." He held out his hand and touched her briefly on her cheek. "Please . . ."

Copper thought about that moment a lot afterward. She knew that if her father hadn't touched her, hadn't said please, she might never have gone with him and then she might have been shut off from him forever.

"I shall sit here in the oak tree chair," said Cedar, "because I need its strength. Sit there, Copper, in the sandalwood chair. It's very soothing."

Nervously, Copper did as he suggested.

They looked at each other.

"I'm sorry," said Cedar. "That's the main thing. I am really sorry that I am just about the worst father a girl could have. I'm sorry for everything, and if you can ever forgive me, I will try to do better."

Copper didn't know what to say. She stared at her father. He was so tall and thin and awkward-looking. So shy and anxious with such pleading eyes, and the way he leaned toward her, his long fingers covering his knees like the roots of a tree clutching a rock, was endearing. She recognized herself in him. She recognized the need to be wanted.

"I'm sorry too," she said shyly.

"You don't need to be," said Cedar, dropping down onto his knees and taking her hands in his. "I've failed you and you've done nothing wrong at all. If I'd ever thought you were alive, Copper, I swear I would have combed the world for you until I'd found you."

Copper grinned at him. "Good," she said.

They talked for a long time, and afterward she and Cedar began to be real friends.

Much later that night Copper found she couldn't sleep. She couldn't settle down. She moved piles of clothes from here to there, rearranged the books and her knitting, unmade then remade her bed.

"You can move it all a thousand times," said Ralick, "but it won't sort out your life, you know."

"I know," said Copper, pulling the rug straight. "But it helps."

"I'm tired. My tummy still hurts. Can't we go to bed?"

"Poor Ralick," said Copper, stroking his mended seam. "I'm not very good at sewing. It was the best I could do. I keep thinking about Aunt Ruby and my mother. About how to stop this crazy war between the Woods and the Rockers. It's up to us, you know, Ralick. I don't think the grown-ups have any intention of sorting things out. I don't expect you're going to agree with me, but I think *we've* got to do it!"

21. An Extraordinary Block of Ice

THE KITCHEN SEEMED crowded the next morning with the addition of the two brothers.

"It will be strange not sending things up in the lift anymore," said Oriole. "And I will have to learn which of you is which."

Cedar winked at Copper. "I'm more handsome!" he said.

"And neither is as handsome as me!" said Robin, laughing.

Copper grinned. "Did you send a message to Aunt Ruby, Robin?"

"I did," said Robin. "The pigeon's not back yet. Still, it's a long way to the other end of the line, and they do go off-course sometimes."

"She said she would come. I know she will."

"Well, I for one can't wait to meet this mysterious person," said Cedar. "She looked after you all these years and seems to have done a very good job of it. I have a lot to thank her for."

Suddenly, the door burst open and cold air whooshed into

the room. Questrid appeared, scattering snow everywhere. His cheeks were red from the cold, his hair stuck up in a mop and he was grinning from ear to ear.

"Come and see what I've found. It's Amber. She's here!"

"What?"

"Where?"

"Here? She can't be."

They jumped up, sending their chairs clattering to the floor, and ran out into the snow.

The lumps of ice that had streamed down the hill behind Questrid and Copper and their faithful boat had collided against the wall behind the house and now lay there like a pile of gigantic empty milk bottles.

But one of them was different. One of them was bluer than the others, with sharp edges and a shine on it like a polished mirror, reflecting the sun with dazzling brightness.

"It is her," Cedar whispered. "It's Amber, my own dear, sweet Amber. It really is. We've got to get her out of this. Think how cold she must be, how frightened and lonely. Come on, everyone, you said she was alive, didn't you? Come on!"

"Calm down, Cedar," said Greenwood, holding on to his brother's arm and pulling him back. "Wait. Granite said only the charm bracelet will get her out."

"Why should I believe anything Granite says? He did this to Amber and I've got to get her out." He ran to find tools to set her free.

First Cedar hit the blue ice pillar with a hammer: it

bounced off as though the ice were solid steel. Then he tried a pickax, chisels, saws, every sharp-edged tool in the house, but nothing even scratched it.

"We'll melt it, then," he said. Everyone helped to gather wood for a fire, and soon a good fierce heat came from the blaze and the snow melted around them. The other ice blocks melted, but the blue ice with Amber inside would not thaw.

"Granite was right, I'm afraid," said Greenwood.

Cedar sank down with his head in his hands. "I can't believe this is happening. To see her there after all these years and not be able to reach her. It's terrible."

"This is the bracelet," said Copper, showing them. "It may help, because it did before and Granite wants it more than anything. Here, take it."

"It's yours," Cedar said. "You try."

Copper patted his arm as if he were a child. "Okay. I'll try the hammer again. It worked in the underground lake, but . . ."

"What?"

"But it's not glowing. In the Rock it sparkled and hummed and was charged with energy."

"And now it's just ordinary," agreed Questrid.

"Try anyway," urged Cedar.

Copper struck the ice with the tiny hammer.

Nothing happened. No chimes. No thundering noise. Nothing.

"Well, try something else," said Cedar. "Try that coin! Try the dog! The babies! Anything!"

One by one, Copper tried each charm, touching or hitting the block of ice with them, but nothing happened.

Cedar jumped to his feet and roared, "I'll get that Granite! He did this, locked her up and stole her from me. I'm going to go up there and fight him and this time I'll *kill* him!"

"No, no, you're not," said Greenwood calmly. "There mustn't be any more fighting over Amber. She wouldn't want that, Cedar, would she?"

"It wasn't Granite anyway," said Copper. "He told me Amber did it herself—she threw herself into the freezing water."

"And you believe him?"

"Why not?"

"Because he's a Stone! A Rocker. He's *Granite!*"

"Amber's from the Stone clan too. Being a Rocker doesn't mean you have to be a liar," said Copper.

Cedar breathed out slowly. "You're right, of course you're right. I just want Amber. I want to see her alive, moving, speaking, looking at me. She is my wife."

Copper stared at the figure of her mother. "I don't think she wants to come out. I think she wants to stay shut away from us all. She's matched her insides with her outside."

"What?"

"I think she was so sad and cold on the inside that she built ice around herself to sort of mirror it. She won't let herself be set free until there is something good to come to."

Copper paused. "Now there's me and I hope she wants

me, but you and Granite have to stop behaving so badly. You have to make friends, trust each other, start trading again."

Cedar made a choking noise. "But I hate him!"

"You have to stop hating him," agreed Greenwood. "I think Copper's right."

"We need to know if Great-Grandfather Ash really did steal that gold," said Copper. "If he did we should give it back. If he didn't we must prove it to Granite. Then he might listen to us instead of trying to fight us."

"I'm not giving anything back to him," said Cedar, then held up his hand in apology. "Sorry. Sorry. I know—how will we ever get anywhere if I carry on like this? I will try to be better, I promise."

Copper flung herself onto her bed.

"I have to go back to the Rock."

Ralick nearly jumped out of his furry skin. "You *are* joking!"

"Ralick, I *have* to. Cedar and Greenwood are just not the type to get things done. They'll never do anything, or if they do, they'll do the wrong thing. I have to talk to Granite and make him see reason. If I could get him to come down here and talk to Cedar and explain how he feels, then I think maybe the charms will start to work to get Amber out. What do you think?"

"I think I want to stay here."

"Oh, please come, Ralick. I need you."

"I'm not up to it. I'm all undone. I need major surgery."

"Ralick?"

"Oh, all right then. But this time no hat."

Copper knew there was no point in getting her father's

permission to go. She knew he'd say no, they all would, so she wrote a note telling them what she was doing and left it on her bed. Then, when everyone was settled down for the night, she crept out.

It was dark, but the moon was full and bright. The snow was a glitter of blue and silver, the shadows black blots of ink.

"Aren't you frightened?" gasped Ralick from inside her coat.

Copper shook her head. The air was crisp and dry, and all around her the still night seemed to be waiting for her. She wasn't afraid.

"I've got the bracelet. I've got you. I'm going to settle this quarrel forever and get my family back."

She set off across the snow. The only noise was the crunch beneath her feet and the soft sound of her breath in the still night air. I will do it, she told herself. I can do it.

When they finally reached the Rock, Copper's resolve began to slip away, as if it were melting and sliding out of her boots. She trembled as she stared up at the bleak, cold fortress, feeling very small and hopeless and cold.

The Rock showed a silent face: the shutters were all locked tight, the door bolted. A tiny stream of smoke trickled out of the chimney. The green light lingered and hung around the Rock where it seeped out through the cracks in the windows.

"Well, I can't go home again," said Copper. "I suppose I'll just have to knock on the door."

So she walked up to the massive front door, which, in hard silver moonlight, was more crumbling and rotting than she'd first realized; the great rusty nails and metal crossbars were the only things holding it together.

With a trembling hand she pulled the iron bellpull. From deep in the Rock she heard it clang faintly. A few minutes later, a smaller door within the vast one opened and Grit appeared.

"What, you?" he grunted. "Coming back for more punishment? You must be mad. Come in, come in. Granite will be delighted to see you."

He let her in and took her to a room where Granite and a large group of men and women were eating and drinking. A fire was roaring in the grate, and on the table were some meager scraps of food. There were tall glass flagons of red wine and large pewter mugs full of frothing beer.

"What have we here?" cried Granite, slamming down a silver goblet. He twisted his bent body round and stared at Copper intently. "Could it be a Wood in our midst? A stick? A twig?"

"I'm only half a Wood, if you remember. The other half is Stone, so I have just as much right to be here as any of you."

The men burst out laughing, banging their mugs on the table.

"She's definitely got some Rock in there!" someone cried.

"Marble in her veins," another shouted.

Granite wasn't pleased. "What d'you want?" he demanded.

Copper took a deep breath. "I came to ask you to make peace. I want to get Amber out of the ice. I want things to be settled. You need wood, we need metal tools and gold too . . ."

"You need GOLD!" roared Granite. "What about the cart-load your great-grandfather stole, eh? Wasn't that enough? Have you finished spending that yet? You surely aren't expecting me to make a deal with a bunch of robbers!"

"I'm sure he didn't steal . . . ," began Copper.

"And I'm sure he did!" shouted Granite.

The Rockers cheered in agreement.

Copper was heating up in her coat, and her cheeks felt hot and red. How was she ever going to make them take any notice of her?

"Please listen," she began again. "I promise we'll try to find out exactly what happened to Great-Grandfather Ash, and if he did steal the money, we'll pay it back, every penny, and if he didn't, well then, that's okay."

Granite walked lopsidedly over to her and grabbed her arms. "Okay? Okay? What do you know about anything? Okay that the Woods have everything? Amber and the charm bracelet? Okay to send a stick child up here to me? Phah! You don't understand anything!"

Copper opened her mouth to speak, but Granite shouted her down: "They're using you. Lying to you. They want Amber, sure, but not because they love her. Not because she's kind or sweet." He pushed his face close to hers, smiling as she squirmed under his gaze. "They want her because

Amber is special. She was very like you, you know, she loved *click clack* knitting and *in out, in out* crochet work, all kinds of needlework. . . ."

The crowd laughed and cheered. Copper stared round at them, perplexed, unable to see the joke.

"So?" she whispered.

"So, so, Amber had a very special way of knitting. Really, most special . . ."

Again the Rockers roared with laughter, thumping their hands on the tables and hooting like animals.

Granite lowered his voice and said, "Amber used her needles to MAKE GOLD."

Make gold?

Make *gold?* The words didn't make sense to Copper.

"What do you mean?" She stared unhappily at everyone, at their open, laughing mouths and unfriendly eyes, and suddenly the room dipped and shifted, as if she were on the deck of a boat.

Make gold?

"What do you mean?" she whispered again.

"I mean she *made* gold. With her knitting needles. I don't know how, but you only had to give her a lump of rock and she did it. She could make gold, *knit* gold out of stone. Extraordinary, eh?"

The Rockers cheered their agreement.

"She would stroke the rock or trickle tiny bits through her fingers, feeling it, searching for the vein of gold inside. Then she'd knit it out. The finest gold you've ever seen."

It went quiet. Copper felt all eyes on her.

"So that's why you want her," she said quietly. "No wonder you hated it when she left. You didn't love her at all, you just wanted to keep her here so she could make you lots of gold."

"No. No. That's why *they* want her at Spindle House," Granite insisted. "To make gold for them."

"No," she said, but without conviction.

Why didn't Cedar tell me? she wondered. Did he know? Was he trying to hide it? And is the whole bizarre story true anyway? Can Granite tell the truth?

Copper tried to look into Granite, for the answer that was surely there in his eyes. All she could see were the misty features of her mother, deep in the ice, and all she could think was how cold her mother must be—so cold, so much colder than Copper could ever imagine—and how unhappy she must have been.

Then Granite's face reemerged and it seemed to Copper that the black letters on his cheek spelled out a new word now: GREED.

"You're lying," she said. "My father loves her. It's not true."

Granite grinned, then looked puzzled, his smile slipping off his face in bewilderment. He looked at the others, then back at Copper.

"Did you say father? What has your *father* got to do with it?"

"Yes. He's down there at Spindle House right now!" said Copper triumphantly.

Granite turned his hard gaze on the Rockers.

"Is this true? Is he there? Tell me!" he demanded.

"The other night, when they came looking for the girl . . . ," someone ventured to say.

"It was so dark," said another.

"Well, well," said Granite. "Alive . . . I'll make sure I *do* kill him this time. He won't get away again. Here, take this stick away! She seems to like it here, so lock her up and throw away the key. We'll keep her."

"You can't!" Copper cried as three men took hold of her roughly and quickly whisked her away. "Stop! You can't keep me! Let me go!"

The men were deaf to her pleas. They half carried her down the steps and into the depths of the house where the cold seeped right into her bones and her breath showed in a frosty cloud. They thrust her into a cell, shut the steel door with a clang and left her alone in the dark.

23. Locked in the Rock

Copper stood very, very still, breathing heavily and listening to herself breathing. She blinked three times, hoping the blackness around her was some sort of illusion. It wasn't.

"Sorry, Ralick," she whispered at last.

"It's all right, clever clogs," whispered Ralick. "I was proud of you."

"I had the charm bracelet in my pocket all the time, but I don't suppose it's much use to Granite now that Amber's down at Spindle House."

She pulled out the bracelet and was amazed to see that it glowed like a lantern, casting a golden sheen around the cell.

"Ralick," she whispered, "it's working again."

"Huh, now I can see what another great place you've brought us to," he said. "I do like the iron wrist chains on the wall. Wonder if we have to pay extra for those."

"Horrid," agreed Copper with a shudder. "But don't worry. They can't keep us here forever. Granite just wants to try to scare me."

"And it's working," growled Ralick.

"No, no. I'm not scared."

"I am."

Copper held the bracelet up and looked around the room. It was a square prison cell, with four small metal doors and no windows.

"Let's investigate," said Copper, going toward a door. "There must be a way out."

"Must we?" whimpered Ralick. "It might be worse out there."

The first door that Copper tried was open. "That's odd." She went over and tried the next. That was open too. They all were, and each led to a narrow, winding corridor.

"No thanks," said Ralick. "I'm not going down there. We'll get lost."

"But we can't just stay here. We must try one. Come on, Ralick. Eeny, meeny, miny, mo, catch a teddy by his toe . . ."

She stopped suddenly: "Did you hear something, Ralick?"

"Yes, shut the doors!"

"Shh, listen. It's an animal, crying. Where's it coming from?" She moved round, listening at the four doorways. "Here, down here."

She paused beside the open door, goose pimples dancing up and down her spine. "What shall I do?" she wondered.

"Stop squeezing me, for a start," hissed Ralick. "I'm going to pop my new stitches."

"Sorry. What can it be? Shall we go and see?"

"No, no, choose one of the other doors," cried Ralick. "Ignore it. Can't you learn to ignore things, Copper Beech? Leave well enough alone and all that. It'll just be trouble, Copper. COPPER!"

But Copper was drawn toward the whimpering noise as though it were her name being called. She crept through the doorway and down the narrow tunnel toward it.

"We can't ignore it, it's an animal in pain," she said.

"Like me," groaned Ralick.

At the end of the long passageway was a small room. The noise was coming from this room, but it stopped as they went in.

Copper waited, took a deep breath, then, holding the gleaming bracelet in front of her, lit up the room.

Copper gasped. "It's Silver. They've locked her in a cage!"

Or it had been Silver. Now it was a dirty, black, smelly and crumpled creature. But the eyes pleading for freedom were definitely Silver's eyes.

"You poor, poor thing."

Copper reached out to her, then stopped. It was Silver that had led the men to Copper the first time—Silver the traitor.

It didn't matter. Silver would die if Copper left her. Quickly she slid back the bolt. Silver slunk out and wound herself round Copper's legs, thrusting her nose into her hand, licking her and whining.

"Poor thing. She's so dirty and thin. What about your babies, Silver? Where are your pups?"

In reply, the big animal caught hold of Copper's coat in her mouth and pulled.

"Where? That way? I'm coming."

"Do we have to?" said Ralick. "It's even darker down there. What if it's another trap?"

"Trust me. Trust my instincts."

"You must be kidding!" yelped Ralick.

Copper let Silver lead her through an archway where there were six or seven other barred cages. Things shifted uneasily inside them, whining, snorting and growling.

"Don't let go of me in here!" said Ralick nervously.

"I won't. I'm trying not to look . . . there's sad things, horrid things."

Silver led Copper to the last cage, where some baby animals, balls of scraggy fur all rolled up together, lay in a hollow of straw.

"Her cubs, I think. So we were right: they stole her babies and then Silver had to do what Granite wanted . . . but they tricked her and locked them all away. Oh, dear, Silver . . . ," said Copper, peering in more closely. "I don't think . . . they're not moving."

Copper quickly undid the bolts on the cage and put her hands out to the cubs.

"They're dead," said Copper. "They're cold."

Silver threw back her head and howled. The terrible noise echoed round and round the cave. Creatures trapped in the other cages whined and whimpered. But Silver wouldn't believe the cubs were dead, and thrusting her nose into the curled-up bundles of fur, she sniffed and snuffled. Suddenly Copper saw a tiny movement.

"Let me help," she whispered. She scooped out a furry ball that bleated weakly and struggled feebly in her hands. Silver licked it and it wriggled a bit more. "Alive. Thank goodness. How could Granite do this?" hissed Copper, stroking the cub. "We'll have to take it with us, Ralick, so it'll have to come down my coat with you."

"Oi, what's going on?" said Ralick. "It's scratchy. It's cold. It's trying to suck my nose."

"It's a baby, Ralick, be nice to it," said Copper.

"Grrr," said Ralick.

"Well, at least I've accomplished something," said Copper, patting Silver's head. "Now I suppose we'd better try to go home. Home, Silver. Which way?"

Silver trotted off down a narrow corridor, turning back to make sure Copper was following.

Just for a second, doubt filled Copper's thoughts as she followed Silver—surely it wasn't a trap? But then she felt the little cub on her chest and knew it wasn't. Silver is good and kind, she told herself. I know.

The corridor was just a tunnel, its walls and floor made of marblelike glistening damp rock. The light from the charm bracelet lit up a small globe around them. Copper was glad not to be able to see too far ahead or too clearly, because every now and again, soft rubbery things squelched under her boots, tiny scampering creatures ran over her feet and things squeaked in the dark corners. On and on they walked with never a change in their surroundings.

"It can't be much farther," whispered Copper.

"A shame—I'm so enjoying this," wheezed Ralick. "I love hiking underground in the freezing cold. I adore wolflet things nibbling me. I love the dark. I . . ."

"We've got to keep going. What else can we do?"

Then in the distance she suddenly noticed wisps of green light streaking the ceiling and beginning to lighten up the tunnel ahead.

"There's light," she cried. "It's going to be okay, Ralick."

The emerald vapor flowed thicker and stronger as they drew near. It streamed over Copper's head in swathes and trickled over Silver's silver fur, turning her into a ghostly green monster. Soon the green light filled the whole tunnel and was so bright that Copper had to shield her eyes. She held one hand out in front of her while she walked.

Suddenly her hand jarred against a metal grid. She felt it hurriedly, panic rising as she realized that it completely covered a large circular hole in the wall.

"It's a dead end," she said, trying to keep the fear and disappointment from her voice. "No way through."

"Are you sure?"

"Yes. There's like a big grid across. The room on the other side is the room Questrid found where the green light comes from. But I'll never be able to get this metal thing off!"

"Try."

Squinting against the bright green light, Copper laced her fingers into the grid and pulled and tugged, but nothing happened. She shook it and rattled it, but the grid was firmly attached and wouldn't budge.

"I can't bear to go back," said Copper, sinking onto the floor. "It's too far, too dark. What shall I do? I bet Granite knew this would happen. He knew I'd go off down his horrible corridors and get lost. I bet every one of those doors in the cell leads to this place. Why did I come?"

"Because you're very brave and you want your mother," said Ralick. "Now, stop moaning and believe you can do it! Use the charm bracelet."

"Bracelet? Why didn't I think of that?" She took the bracelet out of her pocket again. It was buzzing and crackling. Which charm might help her now?

"Little babies? A bird? A tree?"

"Try them all," said Ralick. "Dang! This wolf cub is driving me mad! Try them all, Copper."

Copper flattened the charm bracelet against her palm, laid it against the grid and waited. Nothing happened.

"Oh, Ralick! What should we do? I feel sure we should use the bracelet somehow."

"So do I. Wave it around! Dangle it about!"

Copper shifted her hand. The bracelet slipped, and as she caught it, in midfall, the bird charm shattered into a thousand brilliant splinters like a tiny fireworks display. A thousand miniature gold birds flitted through the tunnel, swooping and swerving like a shoal of fish in the green air.

"Birds," cried Copper. "Beautiful, tiny birds."

The minute birds settled on the grid like specks of shining dust, locking their minuscule claws around the wires until every inch was covered. Then in one orchestrated move, they spread their wings and pulled.

The grid lifted smoothly from the wall, and the birds carried it away and settled it onto the floor. Then, like a swarm of bees, they rose into the air again. But this time, they flew faster, haphazardly, as if they were mad; they flew straight at each other, and as they touched, they merged and made one, like mercury forming a pool. But each new bird was no bigger than the first and in the end just one tiny gold bird was left. It flew onto the tip of Copper's finger and nodded its head once, as if to say, There, that's done, then tumbled down into her palm, a solid, lifeless charm.

"That was the most wonderful thing ever," said Copper quietly. "Thank you." She put the bird charm back onto her bracelet and went through the opening in the wall.

The green vapor rose in a cloud and billowed round the room, oozing its way up into the pipes in the ceiling and through the vents in the walls.

Copper made straight for the door. "Now we can get back. That way leads to the lake or back up the stairs. We're safe!"

But the door was locked . . . from the outside.

24. THE MYSTERY OF THE GREEN VAPOR

COPPER SANK ONTO the floor.

"Stuck. Oh, I'm tired, Ralick," she sobbed. "Silver, I'm tired. I can't go back and there's no way on. I wish Aunt Ruby was here. I wish I'd never come. I was so stupid. Stupid to think I could do anything. They'll all be worrying. Of course I can't make Granite do what I want. I'm so useless!"

For once, even Ralick had no answer, but Silver, who had been trotting round and round the hole in a restless way, started whining and pawing at it. She barked excitedly.

"What's the matter?"

Copper put out her arm to stop her, but she was too late. Silver jumped into the hole and disappeared.

"Silver!" Copper rushed over, swiping at the thick green cloud that obscured her view. "Silver!"

On the inside edge of the deep hole was a whole flight of steps spiraling down into the green.

From way below, Copper heard Silver barking and calling.

"It's a well. That's the only way, Ralick. I think we're going to have to go down too."

"Tell me you're joking," squeaked Ralick. "We don't know what's at the bottom. It might be dangerous."

But Copper was already sitting on the rim of the well and feeling for the first step with her toes.

"It's the only way. Granite will find us soon if we don't. If Silver says it's okay, then it's okay."

"You trust her?"

"Yes. Absolutely. She's a wolf."

"Did you ever read that story called 'Little Red Riding Hoo—' "

"Shush!"

Copper began her descent, holding on to the rough edges of the well with her fingertips. Once inside, the green light engulfed her. It glowed and was bright, but when it surrounded her, she couldn't see through it, so she made her way down blindly.

Copper counted as she went lower and lower. "One hundred and six, one hundred and seven," she chanted.

The air changed: gradually it grew fresher and clearer, and she guessed she was getting close to the end. At one hundred and sixteen, the walls disappeared and she was walking down steps with no sides. "One hundred and twenty!" She stepped onto the floor of a vast cave.

The first thing she noticed was the green vapor. It was different down here, a thick band of it, moving across the cave from the corner, coiling out toward the stairs like a long fat snake. Copper took three steps toward it and stopped. The vapor was coming from a dragon.

"Oh, Ralick! A dragon, a real dragon!"

The dragon was the size of a baby hippopotamus, curled up asleep, with its long spiked tail wrapped around its body and under its chin. Its skin shone like a fish, silver and blue and green, and was scaled like a fish too. Two spiky wings were folded neatly against its sides.

It lay on a nest of moss, and as it breathed in and out, something metallic clinked softly. Turquoise smoke trailed from the dragon's large nostrils, floated down over the nest, seemed to be sucked through the moss, then emerged a brilliant green color and gathered into an emerald cloud above the dragon's head. Every few minutes, the cloud whirled away across the room and up the well steps as if the well were a chimney.

So this was where the strange green vapor was coming from.

"Reminds me of something," said Ralick. "Dragons, wells, Aunt Ruby . . . Does any of that ring a bell?"

"Glinty! Yes! Aunt Ruby's brother dropped her dragon down an old well. Could this be Glinty? If Aunt Ruby is a Rocker, it makes sense, doesn't it? She didn't drown because there wasn't any water in the well. And maybe the Rockers put up that grid so she couldn't get out! I wonder if it flies."

"Hope not," said Ralick.

"I'll creep past her—that looks like a gap in the rocks over there," said Copper. "I can feel fresh air coming in."

They crept past the dragon. *Clink chink clink,* the nest sang as the dragon shifted in her sleep.

"What's in there?" said Copper. "It looks like moss, but—"

"Who cares?" said Ralick. "Let's get out of here!"

But Copper tiptoed up to the nest to investigate. Beneath the woolly covering of moss, something glittered and shone. Copper pushed her hand in and brought out a handful of gold coins.

"What are you doing? She'll wake up!" squeaked Ralick.

"It's gold. Ralick, gold—it's *that* gold, isn't it? The gold coins Great-Grandfather Ash was supposed to have taken. The missing gold!"

"Well, dragons do have a habit of collecting gold," said Ralick as if he knew a great deal about dragons. "But why cover it in moss and make this green vapor stuff?"

"It could be a smoke signal," said Copper thoughtfully.

"A signal?"

"Yes—to Aunt Ruby, of course! Glinty's been sending this smoke signal to Aunt Ruby all these years, trying to tell her where she is. Aunt Ruby wasn't here so she never saw it." Copper's voice was getting louder and louder. "I just know I'm right. And dear Glinty's never given up hope."

"Shh! I've just about given up hope of getting out before this dragon wakes up," growled Ralick. "Come on."

"But why this elaborate business with the smoke and the moss? That's a mystery."

"Who cares. Come on!"

"I'll take these coins with me," said Copper. "I'll show them to Granite. Proof that we've found the missing money and that Great-Grandfather Ash didn't steal it."

"That's not proof," said Ralick. "Where's the missing ancestor? Where're his bones? The wooden tools he was exchanging for the money?"

Copper shrugged. "I don't know. I just know he was innocent."

She tiptoed past the dragon toward the wide crack in the rock where the night sky showed. Silver was waiting for her.

All around them it was still. The night sky was the deepest navy blue, as soft as velvet, and the stars twinkled feverishly.

"Phew!" said Copper. "Safe!" She took three steps forward, then . . . "OH!"

Her foot slipped from under her and she fell: what she'd thought was shadow was nothing—just space! She was falling. There was nothing to hold her, nothing to save her.

"Help!"

25. THE TRUTH ABOUT GREAT-GRANDFATHER ASH

THE INSTANT SHE FELL, Copper felt something catch at her coat and hold her fast. Her legs dangled dangerously in black nothingness, scrabbling to find a ledge or foothold, but something had stopped her drop into the void.

"Silver!"

Copper felt Silver's nose in her back. The wolf's great jaws were clenched tightly on the hem of her coat. If Silver opened her mouth, Copper would fall. Very slowly and firmly, Silver took one careful step backward, pulling Copper up just enough for her to grab a jutting stone and haul herself onto the snowy ledge.

She lay panting with the snow cold against her cheek, listening to the booming of her heart. Silver pressed her wet nose against Copper's face, and she wrapped one arm round Silver's neck and buried her face in her fur.

"One inch from falling into a ravine," she whispered. "Just one inch away. Oh, Silver, I nearly fell. Thank you."

She couldn't move, but lay there holding tightly to the

stone, scared to let it go in case she slipped backward. As she grew less frightened, she realized it wasn't a stone she was clutching. Under the snow Copper could feel something thin and circular. She sat up and dusted off the snow, digging with her gloved hand. It was half an old wooden wheel with a metal rim, the sort that might have been on a cart.

"They told me Great-Grandfather Ash had a cart," she whispered to Ralick. "But this ledge is too narrow for any cart. If he was carrying the stuff along the top of the cliff . . ." Copper peered into the impenetrable blackness above. "Imagine, imagine wheeling a cartload of gold up there! Maybe the wheel jammed against a stone and the cart went over and he fell over too and died—how terrible."

"Dangerous," grumbled Ralick. "Ravines, narrow ledges, dragons . . ."

"The poor man . . . Then later, Glinty must have gone down, collected all the gold coins and brought them up here. I bet the remains of the cart are down there, right at the bottom of the mountain, and his remains too."

Copper stopped, imagining the awful fall. The crash, the fantastic sight as the gold coins scattered all over the mountainside. The cry as Ash tumbled—it was too horrible. Nervously she crawled toward the rocky wall.

"We must get these coins to Granite! Before Cedar wakes up and sees my note, because then he'll dash up here, putting his big feet in it and making a mess of it all."

She looked at her watch. It was six o'clock in the morning. Soon the sun would rise; already the sky was less black.

"Let's go then," agreed Ralick. "Before this wolf cub eats me alive."

Copper took a few careful steps along the narrow ledge cut into the side of the mountain that spiraled up toward the Rock. It was very slippery.

"I can't see the edge," muttered Copper. "The shadows make it look so odd. It's dangerous. I wish we were home and safe already. I wish, oh, that I was anywhere other than here."

"Be brave," whispered Ralick.

The gold dragged down her pockets like lead weights as she climbed. The wolf cub was hot and hard on her chest. Her legs felt leaden and stiff. She kept thinking about Great-Grandfather Ash and his terrible fall. She was horribly aware of the black space beside her and how easy it would be to follow him down there. She clung to the mountain's side as if held by a magnet.

"Just one foot placed wrongly and I will fall into the dark and be nothing," she whispered to Ralick.

"Then watch where you're treading," said Ralick.

"I'm scared. It's as if that massive black emptiness down there is pulling me over. It wants me to fall. Granite wants me to fall. He'd like me to disappear forever. This was my chance to get things finished; get myself completed. He knew this would happen. He wants me to fall!"

"But I don't," growled Ralick. "Cedar doesn't or Aunt Ruby. And you've still got to save Amber. Remember that."

"I can't go on," Copper moaned, clutching the rock. "I can't move."

Silver stopped suddenly, ears pricked, hackles raised. Copper crouched beside her, resting her hand on her neck as they both listened.

"What is it?" whispered Copper.

The darkness of the ravine was so close, so dense around her that Copper felt she was going to suffocate. She dug her fingers into the cracks in the mountainside, clinging on. "It might be the ghost of Great-Grandfather Ash," she whispered. "Or Granite's men, come to push me off. Ralick, I'm so scared. I'm so scared."

The noises were coming from the cave behind them.

"The dragon woke up," gasped Copper.

They heard slow dragging footsteps as the dragon crossed the cave floor, nails scratching on the rock, tail swishing from side to side. The animal stopped at the cave mouth, blowing and wheezing. Suddenly there was a whoosh as the creature leaped out and soared into the air.

Copper stared into the darkness but couldn't see anything except a flash of silvery green. Then the slow, heavy *shluff shluff* sound of beating wings filled the air as the dragon flew toward them.

"She's coming!"

Copper cowered against the wall, squeezing herself flat against the hard rock. She closed her eyes, at every moment expecting the dragon's sharp claws to dig into her back.

She was right above them. The noise of her flapping leathery wings filled her head, a snort of warm air whooshed as she breathed out, like a hair dryer flying by, snow swirling and floating. Then cold air whipped over her cheeks and just as suddenly, the dragon had passed by and was gone.

"Copper! Copper!"

Someone was calling her. Someone was calling and she recognized that voice!

26. Brother and Sister

SILVER BOUNDED AHEAD, disappeared round a rocky outcrop, then came rushing back again, yelping and showering snow everywhere. Seconds later a familiar figure loomed out of the darkness.

"Aunt Ruby!" Copper ran to her and flung her arms round her.

"There, there," hushed Aunt Ruby. "You dear thing. Here I am, just like you ordered. Oh, those birds, you've no idea. The pigeon was so naughty and went off flirting, that's why I was so long. Look at you. Oh, give me a kiss, darling girl."

Copper rested against Aunt Ruby as if she were a cushion and breathed in her aunt's scent hungrily. "I'm so glad to see you. I nearly fell off the cliff. I've been so scared."

She held on tightly as the dragon flapped noisily above them, sending snow whirling around their heads.

"Stop that, Glinty! Stop!" cried Aunt Ruby, holding on to her hat, but she was smiling. "She didn't frighten you, did she? She came to meet me; after all these years she hadn't forgotten. I told you dragons were faithful animals, didn't I?"

Copper told her how she'd found the dragon.

"Dear Glinty! What a good idea to set up a smoke signal. All those years hoping I'd come. I won't be parted from her again, you can be sure. Now, let's get off this dangerous narrow ledge and away from the ravine. You were nearly at the end of the path, you know. Just round this corner it gets wider and you would have seen the front door of the Rock."

"I can manage anything now that you're here," said Copper, sighing. "How did you find me? Have you been to Spindle House? Have you seen Oriole and Questrid and Amber and everyone?"

"I've seen Oriole and we talked lots. She told me where you'd gone."

"And now what?" asked Copper.

"Now we have to see Granite and get this sorted out once and for all. Families should stick together, you know."

"Families! Are you truly related to me?"

Aunt Ruby shook her head. "Not really."

"I know you're a Stone person," said Copper. "I realized that, but are you . . . you couldn't be Granite's sister, could you? The one who married a Wood? The one who was called Pearl?"

"You've worked it all out, haven't you? My husband was a member of the Wood clan. His name was Ironwood—a dear, gentle man. So I'm a sort of aunt. When he died I came back to the Rock with my son . . . for a while."

166

The ledge had grown wider and wider, and now Copper saw they were coming onto much flatter ground with stumps of dead trees poking out of the snow, and there was the Rock, a black silhouette against the paler sky.

Copper paused, staring up at it. "I suppose we have to go in again?" she said. She rubbed the front of her coat where Ralick and the wolf cub made it bulge out. "I need to get this baby home."

"Baby?" asked Aunt Ruby.

Copper undid some buttons and showed Aunt Ruby the scraggly wolf cub. It mewed and snuffled against Ralick.

Silver came and began licking the cub and whining.

"I see," said Aunt Ruby grimly. "We'd better stop and let Silver feed it, hadn't we?"

Copper lifted the cub out from her coat and Silver lay down so that the little creature could suckle from her. The cub was weak and Copper had to hold it against the warmth of Silver's tummy. As soon as the cub tasted its mother's milk, it latched on to her and began sucking vigorously.

"There, isn't that wonderful!" sighed Aunt Ruby. "We'd better just sit here until it's finished. The rest will do us good too. Here, take a sip of this." She handed Copper a flask of warming, fiery liquid.

"I suppose you always knew she was a wolf?" asked Copper.

"I did. She was Amber's wolf."

"Do you know everything?"

Aunt Ruby shook her head.

"You don't know about the gold in my pockets," said Copper, rattling the coins. "Don't you want to know about it?"

"No doubt I'll find out when the time is right," said Aunt Ruby. "There's no hurry."

When at last the wolf cub couldn't drink any more, Copper tucked it back into her coat, where it went straight to sleep.

Aunt Ruby turned to Silver and laid her hand gently on her head.

"Well done, Silver. Good girl. Now, go home, Silver. Go and tell them everything is all right. Tell them Copper is safe and we're coming soon. Go on!"

Silver looked up at them, her eyes shining again and her nose wet and bright. She barked once and then immediately turned and loped down the hill.

Copper and Aunt Ruby paused at the front door to exchange a look of encouragement, then pulled the long bellpull.

"What a mess it looks," said Aunt Ruby, scanning the broken windows and tattered shutters. "I might have been gone for twenty years, not six, by the look of it."

A face appeared at an upper window, then another poked round behind him. They seemed astonished to see Copper again. Or maybe it was seeing Aunt Ruby that made them stare.

At last the door opened and Grit let them in.

"What's going on? I don't know, I'm sure I don't know," he muttered, and he scuttled off down the damp corridor.

Aunt Ruby marched inside and went straight into the big room where all the Rockers had been the night before. A grubby-looking man was dozing by the smoldering fire and the tables hadn't been cleared. The room smelled of old cabbage and stale beer. The wooden tables were cracked and scuffed, and the chairs had been mended over and over with bits of metal.

"Build up the fire," Aunt Ruby ordered the poor sleepy man, "and bring Granite here."

She pulled off her woolly hat and out tumbled her wonderful, wild hair. Copper was delighted to see a brilliant orange scarf twisted into it and massive glittering green earrings dangling from her ears. The Aunt Ruby she loved and admired.

"Sit down," said Aunt Ruby, sitting down herself in the best chair she could find. "Looks disgusting, doesn't it? How can he live like this?"

Granite came at last. He walked into the room slowly, peering at Copper from his twisted, bent position.

"Well, well, we can't get rid of you, can we . . ." Then he stopped, seeing Aunt Ruby for the first time, and his mouth dropped open.

"*You!* How?"

He sat down heavily, staring at Ruby. "How dare you come here? How dare you . . ." He broke off, his attention caught by a trickle of pale green light coiling from Copper's pocket. "Green vapor! What's going on? What is this? Grit! Gravel! Come here!"

But no one came.

"Sit down and listen," said Aunt Ruby, calmly undoing her coat and making herself comfortable. She straightened her billowing green trousers and pointed a long finger at Granite. "I am still your big sister, Granite, don't you forget that."

"Devilish work, this," said Granite, but he didn't say it very loudly. His eyes darted from Aunt Ruby to the green light, then back again. "You shouldn't be here," he said. "How did you get out?" he added, addressing Copper. "And where's that wolf?"

Copper grinned but didn't say anything. She wanted Aunt Ruby to explain.

"You've had things your own way too long," said Aunt Ruby, her purple eyes flashing. "Things are going to change around here. It's my fault, of course. I should have told Copper sooner, but it never seemed the right moment. When your scouts came searching for her, I knew I couldn't hide her any longer."

"We'd been looking for years," said a voice from the corridor, and Gravel popped his head round the door. He and Grit were hiding. "Pardon me, Pearl, but we were. It was the Marble Mountain dragon over the door that led us to you in the end."

"Ah, the dragon," said Aunt Ruby, smiling. "My mistake again. By the way, I'm Ruby now, Gravel, not Pearl. She's gone."

"All right, Ruby. Whatever you say."

"And I shall be coming back here to live," she told Granite.

"No you're not," snapped Granite, leaping to his feet. "I don't want you here! You can't come back! You've no right to."

"Cedar is . . . ," began Aunt Ruby.

"He's dead!" snapped Granite. "She tried to tell me he was alive but he isn't. That's not him down at Spindle House, I won't believe it. He never came back. He's dead."

"You are quite wrong as usual. He's alive and kicking a lot down at Spindle House. And Amber is there too."

"I supposed she would be. She slipped out of my grasp again. But she's still trapped in the ice, isn't she?" said Granite, grinning. "You'll never get her out."

Aunt Ruby stared at him hard. "We will. But the charm bracelet that she made to release herself won't work. It won't work because of you!"

"Me? I never touched it. You can ask that twiglet over there. She's had it all the time."

"It won't work because of all this hate," Aunt Ruby went on. "Amber won't come out of that ice until we all change and do something to stop this quarrel. This war between the families must stop."

Granite got up and began pacing around the room.

"Look at this place!" he roared. "It's your home and it's falling to pieces, it's dying and all because of the Woods. Of course I hate them. They've destroyed us. Why did you leave us for Ironwood, Pearl? We're different. Stone and Wood, they don't mix. They can't mix. We'll lose our special gifts, we'll lose everything to them. They stole our gold and won't admit it. They're cheats, every one of them."

Aunt Ruby looked at Copper and smiled.

Copper looked at Granite and smiled.

Granite looked puzzled. "Well?"

Copper walked over to him, dug her fingers into her pockets and drew out the gold coins. The faintest wisp of green vapor still clung to them.

"Is that gold? What is it?" cried Granite, taking one of the pieces and holding it up to inspect. He turned it over. "Dragon on the front, pine tree on the back," he muttered.

"I found it at the bottom of the well," said Copper. "Glinty was looking after it. There's a whole pile of it there. Lots and lots. There's a broken bit of cart too. It's the money that's been missing. I know it is. Great-Grandfather Ash must have been going back to Spindle House and fallen off the cliff."

"We've never found anything," said Granite. "Where is this cart?"

"Under the snow. Outside the cave."

Granite grunted. "Glinty! Huh. She's been the bane of my life, lurking down there in the caves. Nobody could go anywhere near the well without her scorching them with her breath. Nobody would hurt her because she was yours!" He glared at Aunt Ruby. "Perhaps now that you're here she'll leave."

"Good old Glinty," said Aunt Ruby, grinning.

Granite grunted. "Huh. Then she started blowing this green stuff about. . . ."

Aunt Ruby laughed. "Don't you remember? Glinty's breath's a lovely turquoise, but when she blows on different things it changes. It goes pink when she blows on tree bark, Copper. Funny, isn't it?"

"Not really," said Granite, scowling.

"And green's my favorite color," explained Aunt Ruby. "Dear little dragon."

"Huh. Well—at least it came in useful when we closed all the shutters." He looked up at the ceiling. "It's fading," he said. "Bring some candles, someone!"

"There won't be any more green vapor, Granite," said Aunt Ruby. "Glinty's stopped guarding the coins. We'll have to get proper lights now."

"Or I could open the shutters," said Copper. "It's very gloomy in here."

"We never open them!"

"Well, it's time to start," said Aunt Ruby, marching over to the window and unlocking the fastening, pushing the shutters wide open.

Daylight flooded the room for the first time in years.

"That's nice," said Gravel. "Look, that's really nice, Granite."

"Oh, shut up!"

"I'm going to take Copper to Spindle House now," said Aunt Ruby, "but I'll be back. You wanted the truth about

Ash and the money, and now you have it. You have no excuses for behaving badly. We can start trading again, we can start having a real life."

"I don't want you here," snapped Granite. "I can't forgive you. I'll never forgive any of you."

"You can't stop me," said Aunt Ruby. "This is my home. Like it. Or leave it."

A faint cheer sounded from the doorway where Grit and Gravel and several of the women were listening.

Just before Aunt Ruby reached the door to go, she said, "Granite, about Linden. Did he ever . . . did you find him?"

"No," growled Granite, turning away.

27. Copper Knows What She Wants to Knit for the First Time

COPPER AND AUNT Ruby slowly walked home.

A watery sun was lighting up the mountainside, and the snow was beginning to sparkle and glisten like icing sugar.

"Now, will you tell me everything?" asked Copper. "I want to know exactly what happened six years ago: where you found me, why I need to forgive you. Everything."

Aunt Ruby put her arm around her. "Granite had kidnapped Amber and she was desperately unhappy. She wanted Cedar, she wanted her real home. Granite was forcing her to make gold for him—he wouldn't let her see you until she'd knitted a hundred ounces each day."

"Poor thing," said Copper.

"Yes. Some people would think that being able to knit gold is a wonderful gift, but it isn't. It's more like a curse."

"Could she always do it? Since she was little?"

"I don't know. She was always very special and could do all sorts of magical things. There are Wood people with those ancient arts too."

"Yes, they can make chairs that send you to sleep!"

"That's right. Well, Amber was very unhappy. She gave me the charms she'd made. She told me they were magical and special. She told me to give you one each year until I didn't need to any longer. She didn't tell me what she was going to do. It was a terrible decision, but she decided she had to stop Granite from getting his way and she threw herself into a frozen pool."

"So that bit was true."

"Granite dragged her out, but already the ice had hardened around her, like a glass coffin. He put the block of ice in a cave near the lake and more and more ice gradually gathered round it."

"I saw it," said Copper, remembering it with a shiver.

"That was when I escaped. I was going to take you back to Spindle House, you see, with Linden. Linden was my dear little boy. He was six then, and you were just four. I knew they would look after you down there."

"Linden was a boy!" cried Copper. "Oh, I thought he was a boat!" She told Aunt Ruby all about the wonderful boat that had helped them escape.

"My husband made that boat," said Aunt Ruby, smiling dreamily, "and I called it *Linden* after my boy. Granite hated it, because Ironwood had made it, but he couldn't stop me from keeping it on the lake. I'm glad it found such a good use. Well, to go back to my story . . .

"The night we ran away—a terrible night! Snow a deep

blanket over everything. The wind making it drift. Bitterly cold. I was carrying you on my back, all wrapped up in a blanket like a cocoon, but Linden, dear Linden, he had to walk. I couldn't carry him too. I just couldn't!" She paused and took a deep breath. "We battled on. The blizzard got worse and worse, the snow was driving into our eyes, we couldn't see. The wind roared. I was almost at the point of turning back, when suddenly, Linden wasn't there. He just wasn't there! Oh, I remember it so clearly! The snow swirling round and round, the wind like a wild animal screaming. I couldn't see Linden. I couldn't see him. I turned back, but everywhere was just the same, just snow and wind. . . . I shouted. I screamed. I called and shouted for hours and hours, but Linden had disappeared. Oh, Copper, I nearly gave up and just lay down in that snow and died, but I couldn't do that to you. I knew Linden was gone forever. He couldn't survive out there on his own, so . . ."

"Go on, Aunt Ruby, go on."

"Then I did a terrible thing. Instead of taking you back home to your uncle, I took you with me. I *stole* you. We got on a train and we didn't get off until it reached the end of the line, as far away from here as possible. I didn't know your father was alive and hiding at Spindle House. I would never have done it if I'd known he was there. I thought I needed you more than Greenwood, especially since my own dear Linden had gone. Oh, Copper, can you forgive me?"

"Of course," said Copper, squeezing her aunt's hand

tightly. "You must have been so sad about Linden, I can understand that. But, Aunt Ruby, poor Linden, what happened to him, do you think?"

Aunt Ruby shook her head sadly. "I'll never know."

Inside Copper's coat, Ralick twisted and turned and whispered very, very quietly, "I think we can guess, eh, Copper?"

At last they arrived back at Spindle House and went straight to the kitchen, where the smell of hot bread and porridge filled the air. Copper rushed in and hugged her father and uncle, Oriole and Robin and Silver. Questrid wasn't there.

Everyone crowded around her, firing questions, trying to feed her and warm her and look after her.

"Stop, stop. I'm fine," she said, laughing. "I'm really fine. I'll tell you everything in a minute, but first, for those who don't know, this is my dear aunt Ruby. She's sorted everything out, and although she doesn't know it," she added, "she is going to meet someone very special very soon."

"What do you mean?" Aunt Ruby asked, laughing.

"Oh, nothing." Copper smiled mischievously. "But there's a person who lives here, in the room above the stable, and I was just wondering . . . would you go and tell him breakfast is ready? He's probably busy chipping at chunks of stone, but I'm sure he'll be very pleased to see you."

"All right," said Aunt Ruby, and looking very puzzled, she went out.

"I don't think she'll be back for ages and ages," said Copper, "not when she finds out that Questrid's real name is *Linden!*"

"Is it? How do you know?" cried Cedar.

"I just do," said Copper. "I worked it out. Now, what else? Oh yes, this: this is Silver's cub and he's peed down my sweater."

Copper pulled out the little wolf cub and laid him alongside Silver in her wicker basket. Silver had been washed, brushed and fed and looked well again. As Copper settled the cub, Ralick dropped out of her open coat and tumbled into the basket.

Copper stared, struck suddenly with the resemblance between them.

"I think Ralick could be a wolf cub too. See, he's the same size and shape. He and the cub have been snuggled up together so happily. A *wolf*—I always wondered what he was."

So it's a wolf on my charm bracelet, she thought. And now I know why Questrid thought he'd seen Ralick before, because he *had,* when he was little and we were both at the Rock.

She kissed Ralick and tucked him in beside Silver. His nose was quite wet from being sucked by the cub.

"Poor Ralick," she whispered, giving him a little squeeze, and when he didn't reply with his usual grumble, she stared down at him anxiously.

"Ralick?"

The little cub was wriggling and nuzzling against its

mother, making tiny sniffling and whimpering noises. Beside it, Ralick lay stiff and straight-legged. The cub looked so alive, but Ralick looked so un-alive—as if the cub had sucked all the energy out of him. Even Ralick's eyes had lost their usual special look. They were glassy, stuffed-toy eyes, not like her Ralick's at all. She tried one more whisper: "Ralick?"

But Ralick had gone.

She knew he was never going to speak again.

Copper couldn't speak either.

I'm lost, she thought, I'm lost without him. This can't happen. She stood up, unable to look at anyone.

"I'll just nip out and, er, get something," said Copper miserably, hoping no one would see her tears. "I left my, er, in the . . ." And she dashed outside.

Ralick had gone.

What shall I do without him? I should never have put that cub in with him, she sobbed. He stole my Ralick. I can't bear it. I can't manage without him. *Ralick!*

She kicked at the snow. She banged her fists against her side.

Dear Ralick, gone. Really gone.

Then, slowly, slowly, another idea began to grow.

The wolf cub would surely have died if Ralick hadn't been there. He kept saying it was nibbling him, sucking him. And Ralick had helped keep it warm, so Ralick had saved the wolf cub.

I'm going to ask if I can have the cub to keep for my very own, she thought. He'll be a bit of Ralick, like Ralick's never really gone. In the same way that Silver belonged to Amber, the wolf cub can be my wolf. He'll be a new Ralick.

She wiped away her tears, and feeling for a hanky in her pocket, her fingers closed on the charm bracelet.

The bracelet!

The bracelet was charged up again; it was warm and buzzy and full of life. It was ready to do something and there was still something very important for it to do.

Copper walked slowly around the ice, staring at the frozen woman inside. Now that the moment had come, she was calm.

She slowly laid the bracelet on the blue ice. She arranged the charms into a perfect circle.

The first one was the dog. But now she knew it wasn't a dog, it was a wolf, both Ralick and Silver . . . and the new cub.

Then two identical babies: Cedar and Greenwood.

The heart: that signified love, everybody's.

The bird: Robin's birds and the minuscule birds that had saved her.

The mountain: that had to be a Marble Mountain.

The gold coin: Copper examined it closely. Yes, there was a tiny dragon on one side and a minuscule tree on the other—Great-Grandfather Ash's gold.

The tree: of course, a beech tree and a spindle tree. All trees.

Knitting needles: did they symbolize the magical ones of her mother's that made gold, or were they Copper's?

And the hammer: like Thor's hammer, thought Copper, the great destroyer. The tool she'd needed to defeat Granite.

The circle of charms was complete. They lay there sparkling and fizzing in the sunlight until suddenly, a peculiar, tiny snapping sound followed by a thin metallic clink indicated that something amazing was happening.

It was the great thaw.

Copper clipped her bracelet round her wrist and took a step back. Hundreds of tiny cracks and lines tracked a path across the glassy surface of the ice. They spread like forked lightning: *snap! crack! ping!* they zigzagged through the ice.

It was happening at last.

Her mother was going to be free. The icy tomb was breaking and she was going to meet her real mother.

And then she couldn't.

I can't, I can't, she thought. I'm not ready for this. She left me. She might not want me now. I might not want her. I can't see her yet.

She covered her eyes with her hands and backed away, getting ready to run.

What if she doesn't want me? What if she doesn't like me?

There were loud splintering noises as shards of ice showered the ground.

I must get away and hide. I can't see her, she thought, turning, ready to run.

And then a voice cut in through her thoughts and it was a voice she recognized, although she hadn't heard it for years and years, and the strong memory came flooding back to her.

"Copper."

Copper opened her eyes. The voice had unlocked some-thing inside her.

She knew that voice and now, when she turned and saw her mother, it was the sweetest thing.

"I know you," said Copper, surprised. "I remember you. Now I remember you."

"I remember you," said her mother.

They stood awkwardly, unable to make a move toward each other.

Copper studied her mother's face, her eyes darting over it, looking at her hair, eyes, nose, cheeks, a face that she'd forgotten and yet was familiar.

"You left me," said Copper. "I wish you'd never left me. I've been looking for you all these years, hoping you were alive, dreaming about you."

She didn't know what to say next, and was surprised at a sudden rush of anger. How could this mother of hers have left her?

Amber stepped forward and tentatively held out her hand.

"But you've found me," she said, gently taking Copper's hand and laying it briefly against her own cheek.

"Yes," said Copper in a choked voice.

"And perhaps it's a good thing. Perhaps you will be a better girl for being without me. A stronger girl."

"Maybe," sniffed Copper. "But I wish you'd stayed with me."

"Have you been happy?"

Copper thought. "Yes," she admitted. "But not quite complete."

Amber nodded. "I do understand, and I'm sorry if you've ever missed me too much or been sad. It will never happen again. Look!"

Their two golden charm bracelets were touching.

Copper felt her wrist growing hotter and hotter. Her bracelet was fizzing again. Granite's gold bracelet on her mother's wrist was beginning to melt: the charms were losing shape, becoming blobs.

"It's collapsing," said Amber, laughing. "Look at the strength of our love, Copper. Our love for each other is doing that!"

"Amazing!" gasped Copper.

They held up their arms and let Granite's gold drip in great golden globules onto the snow, forming a large golden puddle.

Amber picked up the golden disc and handed it to Copper.

"Thank you," said Amber. "I'm free. See how strong you are! See what you've accomplished."

"Was it really me?" Copper asked. "Yahoo!" she yelled. "Yahoo!"

She weighed the gold disc in her hands, glanced at her smiling mother, then took aim and threw it with all her might up into the sky. It flew fast, spinning as it went, shimmering in the sunshine, up and up into the air like a flying saucer.

"It'll never drop!" cried Copper. "It'll go on forever!"

Then they heard the flapping of wings. A shadow passed over them and Glinty shot through the sky.

"Glinty!"

She chased after the gold disc, caught it in her mouth and flew away toward the Rock.

Copper and Amber laughed and clapped their hands.

"There," sighed Amber. "It's all going to be fine."

They turned as a figure came toward them from the house. Cedar, worrying about Copper and sensing something had happened, had come out to investigate. When he saw Amber, he ran to her and gathered her into his arms.

They stayed locked like that for several minutes while Copper watched, smiling and waiting. Then they opened their arms to her and she joined them.

"Stay here and be here for me, please," she begged. "I never want to have to do anything like this again. I need you both. I've been needing you for six years."

"I promise," said Amber and she kissed Copper's cheek.

"And I promise," said Cedar, kissing her other cheek.

Then Copper ran. It was too wonderful and too marvelous and too much.

She ran back to the kitchen and dropped into the rocking chair, picked up her knitting needles and cast on some stitches.

In her mind she pictured Amber and Cedar together and smiled.

Amber was warm at last.

Copper held her needles and waited, but nothing came. No

stitches, no *click clack, click clack.* She stared at the thin metal needles in surprise. This had never happened before.

I can't knit, she thought. Where's my pearl and my plain and my looping the wool over? My fingers just won't do it.

She put the needles down beside her, realizing, oddly, that it didn't matter. It was the same as Ralick going, in a way. It just proved that big things had happened, and nothing was going to be the same again.

A tingling lightness spread from her toes and the tips of her fingers, all through her body. She felt so content: a warm, smiley feeling she had never had before.

I know what I want to knit. Nothing.

Nothing because I'm quite finished, she thought happily. I've got all the bits I need to be complete. Ralick would be proud of me for not *knotting.* This is really the end.

Beside her in the wicker basket, the little wolf cub wriggled and snuggled beside his mother.

"Not the end," whispered the wolf cub quietly. "Nothing ever ends completely, Copper Beech, wait and see. Wait and see."

He grinned, and if Copper had seen it, she would have seen that the expression on his furry face was exactly like Ralick's.